VOYAGES OUT 2

VOYAGES OUT 2

LESBIAN SHORT FICTION

by Julie Blackwomon
and Nona Caspers

The Seal Press

This is a work of fiction and any resemblance to events or persons living or dead is unintentional and purely coincidental.

Cover design by Clare Conrad.

We gratefully acknowledge the following for permission to reprint previously published works:
Julie Blackwomon: "The Long Way Home" formerly entitled "Cat," originally appeared in *Home Girls*, edited by Barbara Smith (Kitchen Table Press: 1983). "So's Yo Momma" was previously published as "Kippy" in *Lesbian Fiction*, edited by Elly Bulkin (Persephone Press: 1981). "Marcia Loves Jesus" was previously published in *Azalea*, Volume 3, September 1980 (Editor: Linda J. Brown).
Nona Caspers: "Tick" was previously published in *Plainswoman*, Spring 1988. "Mrs. Hind's Yard" was previously published in *Plainswoman*, Fall 1988. "Está Bien" originally appeared in *Word of Mouth* by Irene Zahava (Crossing Press: 1990).

Library of Congress Cataloging-in-Publication Data

Blackwomon, Julie.
    Lesbian short fiction / by Julie Blackwomon and Nona Caspers.
        p. cm. — (Voyages out, ISSN 1043-948X ; 2)
    ISBN 0-931188-90-3 : $8.95
    1. Lesbians--Fiction.   2. Lesbians' writings, American.   3. Short stories, American—Women authors.   I. Caspers, Nona.   II. Title.
    PS648.L47B54   1990
813'.0108353—dc20   90-8649
                                                                            CIP

Printed in the United States of America.
First printing, May 1990
10 9 8 7 6 5 4 3 2 1

Foreign Distribution:
In Canada: Raincoast Book Distribution, Ltd., Vancouver, B.C.
In Great Britain and Europe: Airlift Book Company, London.
In Australia: Stilone, N.S.W., Australia.

Acknowledgements

My thanks to Becky Birtha who hand-carried my manu-script to Seal Press, my partner Brenda for her patience and editorial assistance, my daughter Dara and my friend Suzanne who believed in me long before anyone else did, and to Barbara Wilson for being easy to work with.

Julie Blackwomon

Thanks to the Barbara Deming Memorial Fund for its fi-nancial help and moral support. Thanks to a tough writers group: Lynn, Judy, Bonnie, Christina and Lynn.

Nona Caspers

Voyages Out 2

Julie Blackwomon

The Long Way Home   3

So's Yo Momma   12

Marcia Loves Jesus   24

Beechwood Street   31

Symbols   50

Ophelia   67

Nona Caspers

Está Bien   97

When I First Kissed Marsha from the Brady
Bunch on the Lips and the Truth about
Why the Series Ended   99

Chicken-Dyke   108

black bananas   116

Mrs. Hind's Yard   131

Tick   139

The Tutu   142

Spring Cleaning   148

VOYAGES OUT 2

Julie Blackwomon

THE LONG WAY HOME

It is three days after my twelfth birthday and my mother is sitting beside me on the edge of my bed. She is holding a box of sanitary napkins and a little booklet that reads *What Every Young Girl Should Know* and telling me for the third straight year that I am to read the booklet and keep the pads hidden from the sight of Daddy and Leroy. I am hardly listening. I am sneaking furtive glances out the window and patiently waiting for her to finish so I can meet the boys out on the lot for our softball game.

My mother is saying, "Look, you've thrown your pretty dress on the floor." She is bending down to pick it up. It is a white flared dress with large yellow flowers. Daddy bought it for my birthday. I am remembering the party, the coconut cake with twelve ballerinas holding twelve pink candles. Momma has straightened my hair but refused to wave it tight to my head so it will look like a process. Instead she has fluffed up the curls like she does my sister Dee Dee's hair. Momma is serving punch in a starched white apron or just standing around with her hands folded in front of her. When she catches my eye she motions with her head for me to go over and talk with the other girls who are standing in a cluster around the record player. I smile nervously back at her, but remain where I am.

My friends are all acting strange. Leroy, my brother and best friend, has been stuck up under Diedra Young all evening and Raymond and Zip-Zip are out on the back steps giggling with Peggy and Sharon. Jeffrey teases me about my knobby black knees under my new dress until I threaten to punch him in the mouth. I wander out to the kitchen to play with Fluffy, our cat, until Momma misses me and comes to drag me back to the party.

Now sitting on my bed with Momma, she is saying she will have to get me a training bra. I self-consciously reach up and touch my breasts then jerk my hands down again. I hate them. I'm always hurting them when I bump into things and now when I fight I have to worry about getting hit in the breasts too.

"Momma, can I go now? I gotta pitch today," I say. Momma puts her arm around my shoulder and pulls me close to her.

"Sugar, you've got to stop playing with those boys all the time; why don't you go play with Sheila, that nice young girl who's staying with the Jenkins?"

"But I don't know her."

"Well, you can get to know her. She's a nice enough girl and she doesn't know anybody. You can introduce her to the rest of the girls."

"But Dee knows them better than I do."

"Yeah, sugar, but Sheila doesn't have any girlfriends and you don't either, so you can be friends with each other."

I pull away from her. "I got friends," I say. I'm getting annoyed at the conversation, I want to go out and play. I get up and walk over to the window and stand there with my back to her.

"Okay," Momma says finally, "but I've invited the

Jenkins over for lunch after church on Sunday and if you want to be friends with Sheila, fine, if not. . . . " She shrugs her shoulders.

"You gonna make Dee be there too?"

"Yup."

"Can we invite Zip-Zip and Jeffrey?"

She hesitates a moment. "Maybe next time."

"Okay, can I go now?" I am inching towards the door.

"Alright, scoot." She pats me on the butt as I pass her. I am running down the steps, jumping over the last two. Dee Dee who had been listening at the door, says "Can I go with you, Cat?"

"No."

"Why not?"

"'Cause you can't."

With Dee Dee at my heels I reach the vacant lot where we play ball. There is no game today. The boys are busy gathering ammunition—dirt clods, rocks, bottles—for the fight with the white boys from across the tracks. Dee Dee whines to Leroy:

"Leroy, I wanna go."

"You can't," Leroy says.

"How come?"

"'Cause you're too young."

"I'm just as old as Jeffrey!"

"You can't go," Leroy says, "besides you're a girl."

"Cat's a girl," she says indignantly.

We ignore her. We are gathering sticks and rocks and throwing them into an empty milk crate.

"How come I can't go? Huh? How come?" Nobody answers her. We are all walking across the lot. Raymond and Leroy are carrying the ammunition; Dee Dee is standing where we left her, yelling, "I'm gonna tell Momma what you're up to too! I'm gonna tell you're going cross the tracks to fight with those white boys." Then, after a moment or two: ". . . And Cat's got Kotex in her dresser drawer!" My neck burns but I keep walking.

I am sixteen years old and sitting in Sheila's dining room. We are playing checkers and I am losing badly and not minding at all. Her cousin Bob comes in. He is stationed in Georgia and on leave from the army. He says hi to Sheila, ignores me completely and walks through to the back with his green duffel bag in his hand. His voice drifts in from the kitchen, "Where'd the little bulldagger come from?"

Sheila springs back from the table so fast her chair overturns. She yells in the kitchen doorway, "You shut your nasty mouth Bob Jenkins!" The next day we are supposed to make cookies for her aunt's birthday but she calls to suggest we do it over my house instead. I do not go back over Sheila's again unless Dee Dee is with me or there is no one home.

We are in Fairmount Park within some semi-enclosed shrubbery. Sheila and I are lying on our backs on an old army blanket. We look like Siamese twins joined together at the head. The sky is blue and I am chewing on the red and white straw that came with my Coke.

"Cat, tell me again how you used to almost be late for school all the time because you used to be waiting for me to come out of my house so we could walk to school together," Sheila says.

"I've told you a thousand times, already."

"Well, tell me again, I like to hear it."

"If you hadn't been peeping from behind the curtain yourself and waiting for *me* we both might have gotten to school on time."

She laughs softly then turns over on her stomach.

"Kiss me," she says.

I lean up on my elbow, check around to make sure nobody's peeping through the bushes then turn and press my lips to hers. After a few seconds she pulls away. "Man, Cat, I never thought I could like a girl as much as I like you."

"Me neither," I reach out and touch her hand. We kiss again, briefly, our lips barely touching. Then we turn and lie as we were before but continue holding hands.

"Cat?"

"Yeah?"

"I think I'm in love."

"Me too."

She squeezes my hand. I squeeze hers back.

"What would you do if Bob came by and saw us now?" Sheila asks.

"What would you do?"

"I don't know, I'd say 'Hi' I guess."

"Then I would too," I say.

The sun has moved and is now shining directly over us. I cover my eyes with my forearm.

"Bob would say we're both bulldaggers," Sheila says after a while.

"Yeah, I guess he would," I say." We aren't bulldaggers, are we Cat?"

"No, bulldaggers want to be men. We don't want to be men, right?"

"Right, we just love each other and there's nothing

wrong with loving someone."

"Yeah and nobody can choose who you fall in love with."

Sheila and I are in her bedroom; her uncle is standing over the bed shouting, "What the hell's going on here?" He is home from work early. Sheila and I scramble for the sheet and clutch it across our naked bodies. I am waiting for her uncle to leave so I can get up and get dressed, but he just stands there staring, thunder in his face. Finally I release my end of the sheet and scramble to the foot of the bed. Sheila's stockings are entwined in my blouse. I cram panties into my pocket and pull blue jeans over naked, ashen legs. I am trembling. Her uncle's eyes follow me around the room like harsh spotlights.

Later at my house Daddy and I are in the dining room. Leroy and Dee Dee are in their rooms, the doors are shut tight. They've been ordered not to open them. My mother sits on the couch wringing her hands. I sit stiffly forward on the edge of a straight-backed chair, my head down, my teeth clenched.

My father stomps back and forth across the floor, his hands are first behind him, holding each other at the butt, then gesturing frantically out in front. He is asking, "What's this I hear about you being in bed with the Jenkins girl?" I sit still on the edge of my chair, looking straight ahead.

"I'm talking to you, Catherine!" His voice is booming to the rafters. I'm sure the neighbors hear. It is dark outside and a slight breeze puffs out the window curtains. I am holding a spool of thread that had been on the table. I am squeezing it in my hands, the round edges intrude into my palms. I continue to squeeze.

"You hear me talking to you, girl?" He is standing directly over me now, his voice reverberates in my ear. I squeeze the spool of thread and stare at a spider-shaped crack in the wall above the light switch. There is an itch on my left thigh but I do not scratch. Dogs bark in the backyards and one of the Williams kids is getting a spanking. I hear the strap fall, a child wailing and an angry woman's voice.

My father is saying, "Look, you'd better say something, you brazen heifer." He jerks my head around to face him. I yank it back to stare at the crack in the wall.

"You're lucky Tom Jenkins didn't have you arrested—forcing yourself on that girl like that. . . "

"What? What force? Sheila didn't say I forced her to do anything!"

"If you didn't force her then what happened?"

"Sheila didn't say that! She didn't say that! Mr. Jenkins must have said it!" I am on my feet and trembling, and screaming at the top of my young lungs.

"Then what did happen?" my father screams back at me.

I sit back down in the chair and again stare at the crack in the wall above the light switch. Trying to concentrate on it, blot out my father's voice. I cannot. I get up and run to the chair where my mother sits. I am pulling on her arm. "Momma, Sheila didn't say that did she? She didn't say I forced her?"

Momma sits there biting on her bottom lip and wringing her hands in her lap. She lays her hand on my head and doesn't speak. My father grabs my arm and yanks me away. I am enveloped in his sour breath. "Look, I am a man of God and don't you dare doubt my word!" I yank my arm away from his grip and run toward the safety of my bedroom.

"I haven't dismissed you!" I hear my father's footsteps behind me. He grabs me by my T-shirt and swings me around. I lose my footing and fall at the bottom on the steps.

"Arthur, Arthur!" My mother is running behind us. My father's knee is in my chest and he is yelling in a hoarse angry voice. "There will be no bulldaggers in my house, do you understand me, girl? THERE WILL BE NO BULLDAGGERS IN MY HOUSE."

I am sitting, beside Sheila on a bench in Fairmount Park; we are within walking distance of the spot where we used to meet with our lunches on Daddy's old army blanket. The grass is completely green except for one long crooked brown streak where the boys trampled a short cut to the basketball court. The leaves are green save for one or two brown or yellow ones beneath the bench at our feet. Sheila's head is bent.

"I am sorry," she is saying. She is picking tiny pieces of lint from a black skirt. "I'm really sorry but you don't know how my uncle is when he gets mad." I am silent. I am watching three boys I don't know play basketball on a court about twenty yards away. A tall white kid leaps up and dunks the ball.

"I just didn't know what else to do," Sheila continues, "I was scared and Uncle Jim kept saying 'She made you do it, didn't she?' and before I knew it I'd said 'yes'." A short Black kid knocks the ball out of bounds and a fat boy in a green sweatshirt darts out to retrieve it.

"Cat?" Her hand is on my forearm and I turn to look her full in the face. "I'm sorry Cat, I just didn't know what else to do." I turn again towards the basketball court, watch the tall White boy holding the ball under his arm. The fat boy in the green sweatshirt is pulling a Navy blue poncho on over his head.

"Cat, please?" Sheila is saying.

I turn to look her full in the face. "It's alright Sheila, it's alright."

It is getting windy. The basketball court empties and Sheila asks if I'll meet her at our spot next Saturday. I lie and say yes. She checks to make sure no one's looking, pecks me on the cheek, then gets up to leave. I sit watching the empty basketball court for a long time. Then I get up and take the long way home.

So's Yo Momma

We were all sitting down the street on Miss Lottie's newly washed steps when Jaimie came by. I think Nikki saw Jaimie first because she yelled, "Hey Jaimie, bring your ass on down here!" when Jaimie was still almost half a block away. Nikki and Jaimie both play basketball for Southern and have gym and home ec together. But it isn't that they're really that tight or anything. It's just that Nikki likes a lot of attention. That's the way Nikki is.

"If you lived on this block you wouldn't be doing all that cussing all up and down the street," Angela said. Angela was sitting on the top step beside Karen.

"All what cussing?" Nikki said in mock innocence, "All I said was ass."

"See, you think it's funny," Angela whined, "but somebody'll be telling my mother we were all down here cussing and she'll be getting on my case."

"Yeah, beanhead," Sheila chimed in, "Cut out the goddamned cussing."

"Aw shut up, pepperhead," Nikki said cheerfully.

"You shut up, fart face," Sheila said.

I stopped listening to to them squabble and turned to watch Jaimie as she approached the steps where we all sat: Nikki, Sheila, Karen, Angela and me. My name's Kath-

12

leen but they call me Kippy. School had let out early and
we were just hanging out on Miss Lottie's steps shooting
the breeze. Earlier we'd been playing hot cold butter beans
but Karen's little brother Boo Boo kept standing across the
street telling where everybody was hiding. We'd chase
him but he'd run and duck behind the parked cars and
come right back to pester us again. We might have been
jumping double dutch, but the rope was in Angela's house
and Angela's mother was home. If Angela went in now
she would have to stay and finish her homework instead of
waiting until seven o'clock when we'd planned on doing it
together.

Jaimie was holding her left arm slightly above her eyebrows, shielding her eyes from the three o'clock sun. She
must have just left school because she still wore her gym-
suit with "Jaimie" stitched in thick yellow thread across
the front. Her books were tucked under her arm.

Jaimie doesn't come over to hang out with us too often
because she's got a part-time job working behind the
counter at MacDonald's at Broad and Snyder. And then
there's basketball practice. Jaimie plays guard for Southern. She's good too, wiry and fast, a blur of blue uniform
and flashing brown arms. I'm always glad when Jaimie
comes over to hang out with us though because I like
Jaimie a lot. Nikki says Jaimie's a lesbian, only it's bulldagger when Nikki says it, but I don't like to use that word
because my mother's a lesbian—which means mostly that
my mother has a bunch of women friends and works for
the women's bookstore and goes to lots of meetings and
demonstrations and stuff, and the only men who get invited to our house for dinner anymore are Grandpop Jones
and Uncle Ralph. Only Uncle Ralph isn't really my uncle
but the man Mom lived with for ten years. Before she decided she liked women better than men.

"Least my family ain't so poor we gotta eat roach sandwiches," Nikki was saying now. Nikki had an unsharpened yellow pencil behind her left ear. She was sitting on the third from the bottom step and was turned sideways with her back to me, looking up at Sheila who was leaning against the wall beside the steps.

"Least we don't drink snot for Kool Aid," Sheila said, then looked over at me. I smiled and winked at her. Sheila's my best friend. She and Nikki live over in the projects about five blocks from here, but Sheila comes over and we walk to school together every morning. Sheila used to live in Harlem with an aunt. That's because her mom used to be on junk but she went into the hospital and got herself straightened out, and now she's okay. I taught Sheila how to bust and she taught me how to fight—how to duck and slide punches. I don't fight much anymore because I'm really too old for that kid stuff. Besides, I don't like to fight and I don't have to anymore because I'm strong and proved to them as soon as I moved around here that I've got heart so they don't be messing with me.

"Least I don't have to steal stuff out the garbage can to wear for Easter," Sheila was saying now. Sheila wasn't supposed to have gotten another bust in before Nikki but I'm glad she did. Sheila isn't too good at busting because she starts taking stuff personal and starts denying. When you're busy denying that keeps the conversation on you. To win you gotta forget about defense and just attack. So if someone says your father's a wino, you just say "least my father don't eat scabs" or something like that. It's not fair to say anything that's really true or to talk about somebody's mom 'cause that means you really want to fight. Like Karen's mom's on welfare and Nikki's pop's in jail but nobody every brings that up. Nobody talks about my mother being lesbian either.

"You kids make sure you take all your shit off my steps!" Miss Lottie stuck her head out the second floor window and glared down at us. She had on a gray scarf tied around her head with a bunch of thick plaits sticking out the top.

"Yes Ma'am," Angela said and balled up her potato chip bag and stuck it in the pocket of the blue jacket she had tied by the sleeves around her waist. Miss Lottie kept glaring at us from the second floor window until Jaimie took Karen's empty coke bottle and handed it to Karen. Then Miss Lottie pulled her head back in the window and closed it.

Before we moved to Pierce Street, Mom and I lived in a women's collective in West Philly. A collective is a house where five or six women shop for food, cook, do laundry and pay bills together just like a family even though some are black and some are white and some have college degrees and make a lot of money and some don't make much money at all. The first year we lived in the collective four of our housemates took me camping at a woman's music festival in Michigan while Mom and Terri went to a black women's conference in New York City. I liked living in the collective. It was like one big happy family. Only most of the family was white. Shortly before we moved here I got into this rift with this kid and ended up calling his mom a black dog. And it had nothing to do with bad feelings about being black either. It's just that when somebody busts on you and you aren't friends with them or anything, the best thing to do is to bust back on their mom—either that or punch them in the mouth. Because if you don't the kid'll think you're chicken and they'll keep messing with you until you prove you aren't. So when the kid called me a black dog I just said, "Your mom's a black dog!" just like that, I mean, it was automatic. But I knew I shouldn't have said it. The moment the words passed my lips I got this strange uncomfortable feeling and when I looked across the street and saw Mom and Terri standing in the doorway I could have just squeezed through a crack in the pavement. I expected Mom to start bombarding me with books on Sojourner Truth and trips to the Afro-American History Museum again but she didn't. I thought the thing was over until about a month later she started talking about me moving in with Grandma and I said I didn't want to unless she went too. Then Mom said although she and Grandma loved each other they could never live in the same house again. But that I needed to live in a black community and she needed to live in a lesbian feminist community. We compromised by moving here which is three blocks from Grandma. Mom still spends a lot of time at the collective house, especially when they're doing layout for the newspaper and sometimes we have meetings at our house. I don't get to go to many women's conferences and stuff with Mom anymore but I still like it here. It's fun spending time with Grandma and Karen lives across the alleyway from me. Karen's the first person I met when I moved over here. Sometimes she spends the night over my house. I can never spend the night over hers because there's no room. She's got six sisters and brothers.

Anyway, after Sheila and Nikki finished busting on each other Nikki went back to the story she was telling before Jaimie came up. Nikki was standing on the sidewalk now with her foot on the bottom step and she was telling us about the lady who rents a room in her mother's house. Nikki's always telling the woman's business. This time she was saying the woman boarder and some man were in the room with the door locked "doing it."

"How do you know the door was locked?" I asked.

You gotta check Nikki's stories sometimes, keep her honest.

"Whenever the door's closed it's locked," Nikki said as if she were talking to a four year old.

"So how'd you know they were doing it?" I persisted.

"Well, what else could they have been doing in there with the door locked?" Nikki said.

Then Karen interrupted to say that yesterday Boo Boo was outside on the steps blowing up a rubber.

"What's a rubber?" Angela asked, and everyone started to laugh. Sometimes I feel sorry for Angela. She's kinda quiet and has really short hair that she hardly ever combs so that sometimes it beads up into little knots and it usually takes her a long time to figure out when somebody's putting her on. They were calling her Pepper for almost a year before she put it together that Pepper was short for pepperhead. Mom says that sometimes black people don't comb their hair it's because they're getting in touch with another part of their ancestral heritage and that's called dreading or wearing dreadlocks but when I told the kids on Pierce Street that, they just laughed and said that might be true for some people but that Angela just wasn't into combing her hair.

Anyway, Karen was saying that everybody was busy laughing at Boo Boo who was outside on the steps blowing up a rubber until her older brother came home, hit Boo Boo up side his head and snatched the rubber. Then when Karen started teasing him about it the older brother lied and said the rubber wasn't even his. Man, it was really funny the way Karen was telling it—she was running back and forth, first being Boo Boo in his high-pitched whiny voice and then her older brother in a deep growly voice. I'm sure she was making some of it up but that's probably why it was so funny. Karen can really make you crack up.

Then we got to talking about who'd seen a rubber and who hadn't. Everyone said they'd seen one, even me, although I hadn't really. But it was okay though, because I had seen a penis—or two if you want to count the Christmas when Uncle Ralph still lived with us and the bottoms of his old red pajamas came loose. The other penis I saw just last summer. It belonged to my cousin Kenny who's fifteen and just starting to shave. I was helping him pick corn in my Grandfather's cornfield in Virginia when Kenny just pulled it out and peed as if I wasn't even there. I turned my head at first then sneaked another peek. Kenny looked over his shoulder and said, "What you looking at, squirt?" Then he laughed and shoved it in his pants and went back to picking corn.

The sun had gone down and the steps were getting chilly under my butt. I wanted to go home and get my jacket but I didn't want to leave because it was getting late and everybody would be going in for dinner soon anyway. Besides, Jaimie might be gone when I got back. So I just got up off the chilly steps and jumped around on the sidewalk a little. I was trying to work up enough nerve to ask Jaimie if I could put on her jacket which was still lying on the steps on top of her books, but before I'd gotten it together to ask, Karen had picked it up and draped it across her knees without even asking Jaimie if it was okay first.

Then somebody started talking about doing it and nobody was saying much because Karen was doing most of the talking and Karen's a real smart ass. Karen'll tell you a really good story, let you tell one, then turn around and say hers wasn't true at all and that she'd only just now made it up. Then she'd crack up. She's a real comedian.

I think Jaimie was getting restless. She put on her jacket which she'd taken back from Karen and was standing around with her hands making lumps in her jeans like she was ready to go. I was getting annoyed with myself because I hadn't said anything at all to Jaimie except "hello," and then Nikki startled me by calling my name.

"Hey Kippy," she said, "Some dude's going into your house." I followed the direction of her gaze and sure enough, someone was standing on my steps and leaning on the railing with their back to us. From the distance I couldn't tell who it was at first but then I recognized Terri's pea jacket and white tam.

"So what?" Angela said. "You a newspaper reporter or something?"

"Ain't nobody even talking to you, Angela," Nikki said.

"That ain't no dude anyway," Karen said with a little giggle, "that's a woman."

"That's a dude, Nikki,"

"That's a woman, stupid," Angela said.

Nikki turned to me. "Ain't that a dude on your steps, Kippy?"

"Terri ain't no dude," I said.

"Well if it ain't no dude it's got to be a bulldagger," Nikki said.

"And what's a bulldagger?" I asked sarcastically.

"You don't know what a bulldagger is?" Nikki giggled and elbowed Karen in the ribs.

"No, what's a bulldagger?" I said, my hands on my hips, my nose now only inches away from Nikki's.

"A bulldagger's a freak."

"And what's a freak?"

"A freak's a woman who wants to be a man."

"Well Terri doesn't want to be a man, she doesn't even like men."

"Then why does she dress like a man?"

"She doesn't dress like a man, she's just got on pants. Everybody wears pants."

"Right," Nikki said, "Everybody wears pants— including bulldaggers."

Somebody snickered and Karen said, "Nikki, why don't you shut up?"

"You shut up," Nikki said without turning to look at Karen.

The other girls were now in a circle around us and Boo Boo and some of the younger kids who'd been playing down the street had now come up to stand around and watch.

"Your mother wears pants," I said.

"Yeah, my mother wears pants, but my mother's got a boyfriend too."

Nikki looked over at Karen, then quickly back at me. Karen looked down at her feet. Suddenly it dawned on me. We weren't talking about Terri; we were talking about my mother.

"Look," I said slowly—I felt sad and kinda tired. "Just because you don't have a boyfriend and don't wear pants doesn't mean you want to be a man. . . . "

The words trailed off and stopped. I wanted to add, "Yeah, my mother's a lesbian but she isn't a bulldagger; she doesn't want to be a man." I wanted to say, "Yeah, Terri's a lesbian and most of my mother's friends are lesbians but there's nothing wrong with that—it doesn't mean anybody wants to be a man." But it just didn't seem right to say it right then and there in front of Nikki with all the other kids gaping on and probably agreeing with Nikki that lesbians and bulldaggers are the same thing when it isn't that way at all. But I didn't know how to make them understand that it was really okay. And I felt kinda dumb and stupid because I didn't know how to make them see.

And I felt disloyal to my mother, kinda like I'd feel if I were high yaller and in an all-white class and someone said something nasty about blacks and I didn't say anything back. And then I was really mad at Nikki all over again because I felt like she'd busted on my mom on the sly and because I was scared I was gonna cry right there in front of everybody and it was all Nikki's fault. I wanted to punch her in the mouth but she was skinny and I knew I could beat her. I wanted to call her a barrel of blitzing bitches but then I didn't because Mom says it isn't nice to call girls and women bitches. But mostly I wanted to anyway because I was really mad and sometimes when you're really mad at someone, calling them a few bitches or motherfuckers is as good as a swift rap in the mouth—though I don't usually cuss unless I'm really mad or just showing off. And now I was just standing around with my teeth clenched trying to decide what to do. And my left leg was trembling so bad I was afraid someone would see it and think I was trembling because I was scared and not just because I always tremble when I get real mad. But before I decided what to do I heard Jaimie's voice from behind me.

"Nikki, why don't you just shut your face and go home."

"This is a free country!" Nikki said.

"Look, Nikki," I said totally ignoring Jaimie's interference, "You and me can go settle this in the schoolyard!" I took off my sweater and threw it to the sidewalk.

Nikki hesitated then took a step backward. "You better get out of my face, girl," she said.

"It ain't your face I'm interested in," I said, both hands on my hips and patting my foot. "I'm gonna kick your narrow butt."

"I don't want to fight you, Kippy."

"Oh you want to fight me alright. Sounds like you

want to fight me real bad." I inched up closer until I was right up in her face. Her nose was blurred from being too close and I could feel her warm breath on my cheek. "Sounds like you'll be thinking I'm some kind of chickenshit if I don't knock you on your skinny ass!"

"I got no reason to fight you, Kippy," Nikki said and she turned and walked away with her nose sticking up in the air like she was the queen of Egypt and I was a mosquito buzzing around her head.

This only made me madder.

"Oh yeah, you want to fight me alright," I said, "You want to fight me real bad!" I gave her a little shove on the shoulders.

"Look, I'm going home," Nikki said without turning around to look at me. She had already weaved her way through the circle of kids behind her. I followed.

"You come back here, you bitch," I said. I grabbed her by the sweater, but she pulled away. I skipped a few steps behind her and pushed her but she kept walking. I wanted to call her another bitch, wanted to go after her, maybe push her again but I was beginning to feel mean, like I was picking on her or something. So I just stood there and watched her walking off with her nose in the air like every one else had disappeared and she was the only one on the street.

Sheila picked up my sweater from the sidewalk and handed it to me and I brushed it off and draped it across my arm. I was still cold but for some reason I didn't want to put the sweater back on. Then Angela mumbled something about getting her butt on home and then she and the rest of the gang kinda wandered off one or two at a time until only Sheila, Jaimie and I were left standing in a half-circle with our hands in our pockets. A kid whizzed by on a bright yellow ten speed bike and I could smell chicken cooking in somebody's kitchen.

"You should have punched her in the mouth," Sheila said.

"Yeah, I should have," I said softly without much conviction.

"I don't know that it would have done any good," Jaimie, the voice of reason, said.

"No, I guess not," I said.

"But it might have made you feel better," Jaimie said. She was smiling now. She has white, even teeth.

"Yeah, I guess so," I said. I was aware that I was agreeing with everything everybody said and for some reason that struck me as funny, so I just bust out laughing. Sheila and Jaimie looked at each other and started laughing, too. I think mostly at me. And then we were all laughing hard, much harder than anything was funny, but for some reason I couldn't stop. It was getting dark and people were walking by and giving us strange looks and that only made us laugh some more.

MARCIA LOVES JESUS

"I've given up women for Jesus," Marcia said in a soft voice that was equal parts boast and apology.

"Oh?" I said.

"Oh yes," she said happily. She was leaning forward on the edge of the couch and staring intently into my eyes. She had her hair pulled back into a ponytail the way she wore it when I fell in love with her in junior high school.

"I've also given up alcohol and marijuana," she added. "I haven't been able to give up cigarettes yet, but I'm down to two a day. One after lunch and one after supper."

"Oh," I said again. I don't think I had any expression on my face. I was trying not to have any expression on my face. I was busy staring at a birthmark on Marcia's chin, near her mouth. Marcia had this cute little heart-shaped mouth that said "Kiss me, kiss me!" At least that's what it always seemed to be saying to me. I figured I'd better ignore it for the time being.

"You aren't upset are you?" she asked.

Upset? Was there a reason I should be upset? Just because for twelve of the twenty-three years I'd inhabited this earth I had loved this woman, wholly and purely without lust? I had loved her more than anything else in the world, including my mother's sweet potato pie and my Stevie Nicks albums. I had loved her with the pure,

chaste, stupid love of a thirteen year old through such di-
verse obstacles as Marcia's thing for Benjie Morris, the
cross-eyed child genius who won all the spelling bees in
the ninth grade; through her passion for Hank Matthews,
the hot-handed All-American fullback who leaked semen
all over my sleeping bag the summer Marcia and I were
supposed to have gone camping alone. Through her all-
consuming affection for Miss Davis, whom Marcia lusted
after through her freshman and junior years at Howard.

Was I upset? Was I upset because Marcia, her suitcase
beside her, was sitting before me in my living room saying
for the third time in ten minutes that she was giving up
women for Jesus? Was I upset? I, who for love of Marcia,
had routinely blown my adolescent allowances on Baby
Ruth candy bars and ice cream sandwiches which I presented to her as proof of my undying love for her—
without strings attached? I, who had stayed up all night
consoling Marcia while she whimpered because Hank
hadn't liked the potato salad she made for the senior class
picnic? I who, that same night in a Herculean display of
compassion and unrequited love, charged downstairs into
the empty kitchen where I ate the entire contents of the potato salad bowl to prove Hank didn't know what he was
talking about? I who got diarrhea for my efforts and did
not complain when I missed the junior prom, (which
meant I could not double date with Marcia and thus prevent her from getting drunk and losing her virginity to
horny Hank, who was not only undeserving but would
never love her as much as I did).

Was I upset? You're damned right, I was upset! Besides,
at this very moment, neatly folded in a rear left hand
pocket of my jeans was a dog-eared letter postmarked the
Ivory Coast. The letter read in part: "I love you woman. I
realize that now. Although it took me nearly ten thousand

miles of distance and a near marriage to an Ivorian sheik who offered me twelve oxen and all the comforts of a house shared with three other wives to become his mate, I realize now that would not work. I realize now that I love women in general and you in particular. I joined the Peace Corps to escape both you and myself, but it has not worked. My tour of duty will be up in another six months. I'm coming home. I love you. Please wait." She had signed it "Yours forever, Marcia," and drawn a heart at the bottom with both our names inside. It made my heart flutter just thinking about it.

So there. It was six months ago, but it was all written down in black and white. Marcia Rhodes was returning from the Peace Corps to be with me. Not Hank Matthews, not Miss Davis, not even Ronnie Jordan, but me. Ronnie Jordan was another story. The first time I told Marcia I loved her in that special way most girls reserve for boys, Marcia unleashed her guilt and put her denial into third gear. The things we did in bed at night when we slept over—the touching, the kissing, all that had been practicing for the boys. I could never convince her that boys didn't really deserve us (I never believed her when she said she liked kissing Hank). We were "best friends," she said, like "sisters," right? Wrong!

Marcia's response to acknowledging our attraction to each other was to run off and pick up Ronnie, who happened to be the first obviously gay woman to respond to Marcia's advances. When that didn't work, Marcia joined the Peace Corps and hid in the Ivory Coast for two years. She must have thought lesbianism was a fatal illness and she was hiding out while waiting for some scientist to find a cure. But two years later Marcia said she was coming home to be with me. Patient, constant, long-suffering me. The letter was in the hip pocket of my jeans. I mean I had the evidence, you understand; I was not hallucinating. Only now Marcia was sitting in front of me, wearing a silver cross where I'd expected a double women's symbol to be, and she was saying for the fourth time that she was giving up women for Jesus. And she wanted to know if I was upset.

"No," I lied in my best Joan of Arc voice, "I'm not upset." I chewed the nail of my forefinger down to the quick. "But isn't this rather sudden?" I said finally and mostly to fill the silence.

"Well not really," she said, "there's this missionary who..."

"Ah ha!" I said, springing to my feet. "It's really the missionary isn't it?" Another woman I could understand.

"No," she said with a patient smile. I hated that look, especially when directed at me by someone who'd just poured sour cream into my Kool Aid.

"It's Jesus," she said. "It's really Jesus." A bright halo suddenly made a wide arch and hovered just above her head. I stared at it, speechless. Personally I'd much rather have lost her to the missionary, but this was not a democratic situation and my vote did not count.

"So you're into Jesus," I said and looked up quickly trying to surprise a smile on her face, or some small indication that she was only fooling.

"Well, yeah," She looked down at her fingers now entwined in her lap, then back up at me. "Yeah," she said with no additional prompting. "Yeah," she said a third time, in case I was hard of hearing, I guess.

"Well, I wouldn't put too much faith in such a relationship," I said.

"This is it for me," she said abruptly, rising to her feet. "Something's been missing in my life all this time. Some vital ingredient just was not there."

"Yes, you fool," I said, "But it was me. Me!"

"You know what it was like?" she asked, ignoring my inspired outburst. She paced up and down in front of the couch wringing her hands, "It was like making love and never reaching orgasm." Now she had the nerve to blush. "You know," she said, "It was almost like... "

"Yeah, it was like sleeping with Hank," I said irritably.

"Well, yeah," she conceded.

"It's going to be that way with Jesus, too," I said. "Men always get caught up in their own gratification."

"I've given up things of the flesh," she said, "Orgasms are not important."

"You get left stranded like a hang glider on that high, mossy cliff a few times and then we'll discuss how important orgasms are," I said morosely.

"Jesus is special," she said.

I was cool. I put my cigarette out on the coffee table and dumped my ash tray into the tropical fish tank. If Marcia noticed, she didn't say anything about it.

"You realize," I said, trying a different tactic, "That Jesus is into slave and master roles? He'll have you drying his feet with your hair."

"I love Jesus, only Jesus," she said, "He's my alpha, my omega. He fulfills all my needs. Knowing I have Jesus has made all the difference in my life." She started tapping her foot as if to some music heard only by herself.

"But this is ridiculous," I said, "I mean the last time you wrote me you were saying.... " I leaned forward and reached for the letter in my hip pocket.

"It was bigger than the both of us," she said, "But now I have overcome. Now I've found Jesus, hallelujah! I've surrendered myself to Jesus, only Jesus. Praise the Lord!"

"But you've always insisted on monogamous relationships in the past," I said.

"What?" She looked at me, confused. I could not keep a smug smile from my face.

"Those nuns—he's married to those nuns in the Catholic church."

"I don't know about that. . . . " she said, but I could tell I'd made her stop and think.

"And not only that," I said, now that I had her complete attention. I figured I might as well go for broke. "He's bisexual at best. There were Peter and Paul, and John too."

"I wouldn't say that," she protested.

"Would I lie to you?" I asked, trying to keep the shrill out of my voice. "You ever hear of him having a girlfriend during the years he was hanging out with all those guys?"

"Jesus is my rock," she said stoutly, "My mountain, my fortress." She was waving her small fist.

"Well," I shook my head sadly, "I guess you know what you're doing, and if you can handle the S and M . . . " I shrugged my shoulders, "Who am I to complain?"

"What S and M?"

"You didn't know about the S and M?" I asked, incredulous. "Anybody who would allow himself to be nailed to two pieces of board in front of a crowd of onlookers has got to be into masochistic exhibitionism."

"But his father told him to do that!" she said indignantly.

"And that's another thing," I said. "The man just can't stand up to authority."

"I don't care what you say," she said, sticking her fingers into her ears and closing her eyes. "I just want to go to heaven and be with Jesus."

"I don't know why you want to go there. There'll be no feminist revolution, no Dos Equis, no Grand Marnier; just you and a bunch of strangers standing around drinking milk and honey—no one you know will be there."

"Jesus will be there," she said quietly.

"Yeah, him, Peter and Paul and about a million horny nuns."

"You too can be there if you repent and accept Jesus as your personal savior."

"No, thank you," I said. "That guy's got a lot of problems and furthermore," I added as I picked up my purse and headed towards the door, twelve years of anger and frustration finally rising to the surface, "I think you're a fickle snot and you and Jesus deserve each other."

"That's not a nice thing to say," she said.

"I know." I jerked open the door and stepped out into the hallway. "But to tell you the truth, I don't feel like being very nice right now. Sometimes, life is hard like that."

"I'll pray for you," she said softly behind me.

"You better pray for yourself, sister," I said from over my shoulder as I headed down the hall, "Because you and Jesus gonna need it."

BEECHWOOD STREET

My daughter, Denise, and her new friend, Timmie, are downstairs in the basement playing chess and listening at full volume to the Blue Notes bemoan "The Love I Lost." They've been at it for several hours now. Occasionally, I'll set aside my typing and tromp downstair—lest I sneak up on them—to take them a snack, turn down the volume on the stereo, or both, and to reiterate my contention that "Nobody can play chess in all that noise!" Then Denise will smile and wink at me and I'll smile too but turn the volume down anyway. My maternal job done, I'll return to my desk upstairs. It is a game we play.

Timmie is my favorite of my daughter's friends, probably because he is tall, dark-skinned, and unusually bright, and therefore reminds me of Ducky McPhearson, a boy who was my best friend when we lived on Beechwood Street in North Philadelphia. I think also that Timmie reminds me of Ducky because Timmie is slightly effeminate and therefore destined to be teased by his peers, although it wouldn't matter in what way he was different.

When I think of Ducky McPhearson, I feel the same bright red ache of pain tinged with guilt that I feel when I

31

recall the first time my daughter caught me in a lie and discovered I wasn't perfect. These feelings occur because my
friendship with Ducky did not end naturally from growing in different directions, or moving away and not keeping in touch, the way I assume Denise's friendship with
Timmie will end—if it ends at all. My friendship with
Ducky ended because I betrayed his confidence. And although it's been almost twenty years since we were "best
friends" and trying to grow up in North Philadelphia in
the late fifties, there are times seeing Timmie and Denise
hunched over the chessboard when I feel the loss as if it
were yesterday.

The summer our friendship turned sour we were both
fifteen and a half and inseparable. We spent so much time
together his mother apparently thought we were "doing
it" and wouldn't allow him to come to my house unless
someone else was home. My mother too wasn't particular
about Ducky and me spending so much time alone in the
house. So Ducky would sneak in through the back door
and leave before my mother got home. This kept everybody happy. They needn't have worried, though. Ducky
and I were best friends and not romantically interested in
each other. He did make a few half-hearted attempts at
trying to get me to close the blinds and sneak upstairs with
him, but that was mostly an intellectual pursuit born of
adolescent curiosity. Because that was also the year of
Ducky's uncle's subscription to *Sexology*. Ducky would
sneak his uncle's magazines to my house where we would
sit around in the living room learning of such interesting
things as premature ejaculation and that sexual intercourse
was the proper word for "doing it." And although I was
interested in sexual experimentation (and who better to
experiment with than your best friend?), I was also an in-
sufferable prude and fervently believed in the good girl,

bad girl, and "guys don't respect girls who give in" mentality as espoused by *True Confessions*. I did, however, once consent to let Ducky see my budding breasts. I could do this with Ducky and not feel the sense of guilt and exploitation that I would have experienced had I done this with any of the other boys on Beechwood Street, because not only was Ducky shy around girls, he was also the block's sissy. Not that he was effeminate or anything. (Earl Brown was the only effeminate kid we knew, but he lived on the corner and usually hung out in the projects across Diamond Street.) Ducky was the block sissy because he didn't like basketball, couldn't fight, and went to Catholic school. Not only that, he played the violin, wore better clothes and had a larger vocabulary than most of the kids. But Ducky's biggest problem was that he usually played his trump card: his sharp wit. This might have impressed our parents or the teachers at the Catholic school he attended, but only succeeded in antagonizing the other kids on the block. They just considered him a smart-mouthed sissy. And since he would seldom fight, any kid who feared losing an argument could silence his quick wit by threatening to punch him in the mouth.

Like Ducky, I too was a virgin at fifteen, and we almost never talked about sex on a personal level. We would read his uncle's *Sexology* and talk abstractly about "Herman the Hermaphrodite" or "Nina the Nymphomaniac" but it was all good, wholesome textbook talk, complete with the clinical terms that even a prude such as I could deal with. It had nothing to do with "real sex" which for me at fifteen was illicit words written on the walls in the school yard. Or coming home from poetry club to surprise girls in my brother's room. It was the only way I could deal with sex, even masturbation, until long after I'd gotten married and divorced for the second time.

One of the few times "real sex" did come up was one spring afternoon shortly before school let out for the summer in 1957. It would set the stage for the betrayal that resulted in the end of our friendship. I heard Ducky's dum dum, de dum dum, on the back door and I yelled from the living room, "C'mon in!" I heard the screen door slam, and when I entered the kitchen, he was carefully placing his violin case in the corner near the table. Ducky was going to be another Issac Stern, and I, an Edna St. Vincent Millay. There was no doubt in either of our minds.

"Hi," I said, "you just getting home from rehearsal?"

"Uh huh." He seemed distracted. I walked over to the sink and ran water on the day's accumulation of dirty dishes which had to be cleared out before my mother came home.

"Guess what, Dee?" he said to my back.

"What?" I said.

"I'm going to get some this weekend."

"You're what?" I asked and pulled my hands from the soapy water, wiped them on my skirt and sat down at the table in front of him.

"I'm going to get some on Saturday," he said. He fished a loose cigarette from his shirt pocket, lit it, then leaned back in his chair and grinned at me.

"You are?" I asked, averting my eyes. I picked up a pencil from the table and doodled my name on the yellow formica top and reminded myself to clean it off before my mother got home from her job doing hair at Charlie's Beauty Shop. Then I coughed and grabbed my throat as if I were choking to death.

"Ducky, get rid of that thing and air this place out. My mother'll be home soon." It wasn't exactly the truth but I needed something to complain about. Ducky walked to the sink, dipped the cigarette in my dishwater, then dropped it into the trash can.

"Don't you want to know who I'm going to do it to?" he asked.

I concentrated on drawing hearts around my name in silence.

"To Dora Johnson," he said finally.

Surprised, my eyes involuntarily leapt up to his face. "Oh," I said and looked down at the table again.

"Oh? Is that all you gotta say?"

"What do you want me to say?" I was embarrassed.

"Don't you think it's about time?"

"It's supposed to be something special," I said, "not just with Dora Johnson!"

"What's wrong with Dora Johnson?"

"Nothing, I guess."

"What do you mean you guess?"

"Well, Dora'll do it to anybody," I said.

"So what?"

"Well," I said, slamming the pencil down on the table, "if you want your first sexual experience to be with someone like Dora Johnson. . . . "

"James Albert did it to Dora," Ducky said.

"Sure, she's done it to Lionel and Bud and Jimmy Shannon too. Dora'll do it to anybody!"

"Dee, you're a Victorian prude!"

"It's your life," I said, sucking my teeth.

"Look, I just want to do it to her. I'm not getting married."

I'd wanted my best friend's first sexual experience to be what I'd hoped my own would be—pure, chaste, and coming after marriage. If not that, then saturated with a lot of masochistic restraint and tears from "going too far" (à la *True Confessions*). I didn't want Ducky to be like the other "nasty" boys on the block. I had great hopes for him. And I think the conversation was not without some jealously on my part. I've always been jealous of my best friend's involvement with other people. I shared Sandy, my best female friend who was in my class at school and lived eight blocks away, but I wasn't used to sharing Ducky with anyone.

"It's your life," I repeated. From the corner of my eye I saw him staring at me in silence.

"Are you really going to do it to her?" I asked after a while.

"Damn right!"

"But to Dora Johnson, Ducky?"

"Do you realize I'm the only boy on the block who hasn't had any yet?"

I realized it, but I didn't consider it important.

My brother, James Albert, was sixteen when Ducky and his mother moved back onto Beechwood Street. His mother had been born there, but she'd married an engineer and moved to Connecticut. They say Ducky and his mom came back to visit his grandmother and uncle at least once a year, usually around Christmas, but although my brother and I had been living on Beechwood Street since I was eleven and my brother thirteen, I recall seeing neither Ducky nor his mom until the summer both Ducky and I turned thirteen and Ducky's mother gave him a surprise birthday party. Apparently only a few of the kids with invitations came, so Mrs. McPhearson finally invited the other kids on the block to finish off the ice cream and cake.

After the party, the kids from the block used to go over to Ducky's house to hang out sometimes. But if we did anything tacky like not flushing the toilet, or not straightening up the couch cover when we got up off it, Ducky's mom would drift into a monologue about how Beechwood Street used to be comprised of doctors, lawyers, and politicians before "other people" started moving in and messing it up. Although it was obvious that "other people" was synonymous with being poor and black, somehow we all knew that if we challenged her on it, she would have found a perfectly rational explanation as to why she wasn't talking about anyone within earshot. So we brooded in silence and pretended we didn't see her when she passed on the street.

My brother, James Albert, however, got his revenge by verbally attacking Mrs. McPhearson on the street loud enough so that maybe she heard it and maybe she didn't. She never confronted him on it, so I suppose she never heard, because a quick call to our mother would have stopped it immediately.

My sympathy at the time was not for her, a woman being hassled on the street by an adolescent male, but for Ducky, because James Albert would unload on her in front of whomever happened to be there, especially Ducky. The code of the street said that if someone insults your mother, unless you're a sissy or something, you have to do something about it. And since Ducky thought it stupid to fight over words, it was, before his peers, more of an insult to him than it was to his mother who probably hadn't heard it in the first place.

On the Friday morning preceding the day of Ducky's proposed sexual initiation with Dora Johnson, Ducky and I were sitting on the steps watching James Albert and Lionel who had just finished playing wall ball. Lionel was leaning against the wall, his cap cocked to the side. James Albert still held the tennis ball they'd been playing with and they were squabbling about whether it required more intelligence and skill to be a quarterback or a point guard.

Then Ducky's mom passed from across the street with her skinny legs in stockings and high heels. She had already passed the house parallel to ours and I thought it would be without incident until James Albert said, without turning to look at her, "Well, well, if it isn't Miss Prissy Bitch coming out for a little sunshine with all the common folks." Four heads turned to spot Ducky's mom as she turned the corner pulling a large shopping cart behind her.

"Aw, you shouldn't be talking about the lady like that," Lionel said. But he had this big grin that clearly said, "C'mon, man, make me laugh some more."

Ducky didn't say anything. He never did. He just stuck his hands in his pockets and walked off the way he always did when James Albert started in on his mother.

"Why don't you lay off Ducky?" I said.

"I ain't messing with Ducky," he said in mock innocence.

"You're sounding on his mom!"

"Well, she is a prissy bitch and someone needs to get on her case."

"That isn't Ducky's fault," I said.

"It's his fault that he's such a punk."

"If he said anything to you, James Albert, you'd punch him in the mouth."

James Albert giggled and tossed the ball in the air. "Yup, you're right about that," he said. He was shirtless and his brand new blue jeans hung so low on his hips you could see the top of his white jockey shorts.

"He ain't got no business hanging out with us lower-class people anyway," Lionel said.

"Nobody's talking to you, Lionel," I said. I decided to

appeal to my brother's sense of fair play. "How would you like it if somebody said nasty things like that about Mom?" James Albert stopped bouncing the ball against the wall, and it now made an awkward looking bulge in his pocket. "In the first place," he said, counting off on his fingers, "nobody's gonna be saying anything about Mom 'cause if they do I'll punch them in the mouth; in the second place, everybody knows our mom's a sweet old lady. Ain't that right, Lionel?" and he suddenly whirled and tossed the ball to Lionel who yanked his hands out of his pockets just in time to catch it.

"That's right," Lionel said and tossed it back.

James Albert winked at me. "Beside, the dude's a faggot, and you can't expect faggots to behave like regular guys."

"He is not a faggot," I said.

"I don't know why you keep defending him, Dee. If the dude's a faggot, he's a faggot."

"He is not," I said acidly, "and you're not supposed to be out here, anyway. Mom said for you to stay in the house until you finish cleaning the basement!"

"Oh, no," he said, wagging his finger in my face. "You can't get out of this by changing the subject. The dude's a faggot and you just have to deal with it. Ain't Ducky a faggot, Lionel?"

"Yeah, man," Lionel said with a straight face, "I didn't want to say anything because I know how tight he is with your sister."

In retrospect, it's hard to imagine why I didn't realize the boys had just found something to tease me about and were running it. It's difficult to explain what faggot or sissy meant—the words in our childhood minds were blurred, imprecise. For instance, although an effeminate man we encountered on the street might be referred to as a sissy or faggot, our main cause for disdain would be because he was "acting like a girl" which translated as weak and ineffective. Having learned our sexist training early and well, nobody wanted to be "like a girl." But it had nothing to do with how one got one's orgasms. By the same logic, the word faggot was interchangeable but reserved for more severe cases like being angry with someone. So, if you were trying to intimidate someone into doing something, one of the guys or girls might say, "If you don't do this, then you must be a sissy," at which point the challenged kid might accept the challenge if he wanted, or say "the heck with you," if he didn't. But they could remain friends with no loss of face regardless. Faggot, however, meant war. It was tantamount to a punch in the face or talking about somebody's mother. In my head I understood this perfectly, yet I allowed the boys to bait me.

"Well, If Ducky's a faggot, then Lionel is too," I said. I didn't have the nerve to call my brother a faggot.

"Look, Dee, I don't play that," Lionel growled at me.

James Albert held up his hand for Lionel to cool it, then turned to me. "Now, just because your buddy's a faggot, you wanna go and call my buddy a faggot too, right?"

"He ain't no faggot!" I said almost in tears.

"Then how come he's almost fifteen and ain't never had no stuff?"

"Because his mother won't let him," I said, mostly to get the conversation safely back onto Ducky's mother.

The boys broke up laughing. "His mother won't let him? His mother won't let him? Did you hear what she said, man, his mother won't let him!" James Albert was holding his side and leaning against the wall, his head down, laughing. Lionel was sort of jumping around in little circles and patting James Albert on the back. I just stood there giving them both my most hostile glare.

"Now if that don't prove the dude's a faggot, I don't know what does," Jay said, after his laughter had dissipated into a broad grin. "Who else but a dumb faggot would let his mother stop him from getting some stuff?"

"I hate you," I said to my brother between clenched teeth.

"You hate me 'cause your buddy's a faggot? It ain't my fault. Now let's see—he can't play basketball, can't fight, don't hang around girls—except... ," he paused and rubbed his thumb against his chest. "Now wait just a minute, maybe I underestimated the young dude." He looked back and forth between me and Lionel, then stopped and pointed his finger at me. "I mean, you and Ducky certainly spend a lot of time together... maybe... " I felt the back of my neck burning. I looked over at Lionel who was grinning as if someone had just given him a brand new Schwinn.

"Screw you," I said, icy and quiet.

"Did you hear that Lionel? The language girls use nowadays is just atrocious. How do you think poor Mom'd feel if she knew her baby girl was playing with faggots and talking like that to her first born too?"

"How do you know Lionel ain't a faggot?" I asked belligerently.

"Because Lionel's had some stuff."

"How do you know? You can't know for sure. Lionel could just be running off at the mouth."

Lionel opened his mouth to reply, but James Albert silenced him with a wave of his hand. "A true gentlemen," James Albert said, "does not kiss and tell." Then he winked at me and elbowed Lionel in the ribs. Lionel just stood there with that stupid grin on his face.

"Well, Ducky's gonna do it too," I said.

"Get outta here, girl." My brother dismissed me with a wave of his hand.

"He is too," I said and hesitated trying to decide which was the greater loyalty—then I plunged ahead. "He's gonna do it to Dora Johnson!"

Around noon the next day, Saturday, the day of Ducky's proposed sexual initiation, James Albert, some other kids, and I were hanging out on Sidney's steps. Sidney was about twenty, an old head by our standards, but sometimes he let us hang out with him. He was the only one we knew with his own car, a hot rod Chevy he called "Baby." One of the girls, Shirley I think, talked him into taking us all for a ride. So James Albert, Shirley, Sandy, Lionel, Bud, and I all crammed into the car and Sidney drove us out to the airport and parked by the hurricane fence where we watched the huge planes taking off in bursts of smoke and noise.

It was a mellow, laid back afternoon, and I was having a nice time until James Albert announced that Ducky was supposed to get his first "piece" today. I yelled that James Albert had a big mouth and James Albert said that it was I who must have had the big mouth because I was the one who told him. Then Bud said something about it being about time. Then Sidney said something else I didn't understand, but I heard Earl Brown's name mentioned and all the boys laughed and Sandy asked what it meant and they laughed again.

Shortly after it got dark, we came back and spread out on Sidney's steps again. Shirley was still sitting up under Sidney but not nearly as close because her grandmother was home from work. I was waiting for Ducky and keeping an eye out for my mother too because my guilty conscience told me that if she heard us laughing she would know I was sitting down there listening to Sidney tell dirty jokes.

Ducky came first, rounding the corner, his white pants and T-shirt glistening in the semi-darkness. He stopped to say something to his grandmother who was sitting on the steps beside his uncle and I got up and eased off the steps without telling James Albert I was going. I went home, unlocked the back door, then came back and sat down on the couch in the living room without turning on lights, other than the one in the front hall which was always on when no one was home. Ducky came in a short while later, through the front door this time. This should have been my first warning that something was wrong. He wore a pair of black sunglasses across the top of his head and took them off when he slumped down in the large stuffed chair facing the window. Light from the lamp sliced through the blinds and made horizontal lines across his arms and shirt. He looked sad and tired.

"Your Mom on your case about being late?" I asked.

"No, I told her I was at rehearsal."

I waited in silence. A T.V. in a window across the street showed two small boxers pummeling each other. The picture snapped and rolled out of focus each time a car passed. I waited some more. After all, that's why he was there, wasn't it? To tell what happened. I waited. Crossed my legs and leaned back on the couch, remembering James Albert and Lionel on the steps across the street. There's no way they would not tease Ducky about this.

"Well, what happened?" I asked when I could no longer stand the silence.

"Nothing happened."

"She stood you up?"

"She was there," he shrugged his shoulders and seemed about to say something else but stopped.

He wiped his sunglasses on his shirt, then slumped back in the chair tapping the ends together with a clicking noise that irritated me. I leaned back on the couch again. My lips were taut. Ducky remained quiet. Fiddled with his sunglasses in silence. I imagined Sidney and Lionel still sitting on the steps across the street calling out to Ducky, "Hey, man, I heard you got some stuff," and Ducky, always a private person, saying evasively, "Oh, where'd you hear that?" And Lionel, not anxious to reveal his source of information saying, "Word gets around." But Ducky would know. There was no one who could have told but me.

"So, what happened?" I asked.

"How may times do I have to tell you, nothing happened?" he said irritably.

"Alright, Ducky, if you don't want to tell me, fine."

He sat quietly, looking away from me with the pouty defiance of a little boy, then finally he said, "I went over there. But I didn't do anything."

"But why not?"

He put his sunglasses on and then pulled them off again. "I'm not sure," he said. "I guess... " And a sudden inexplicable fear gripped me and I didn't want him to tell me anything else. I placed my hands over my ears and said quietly, "Jesus Christ, Ducky." I pushed myself off the edge of the couch and walked over to the window. Bud's father was passing, just coming home from second shift at the navy yard, his metal lunch pail under his arm.

"Jesus Christ," I said again.

"What's the matter?" he said, from behind me. We were both whispering as if we were standing just outside an intensive care ward.

"You don't understand," I said.

"What's there to understand?"

"But you don't understand," I said again.

"What don't I understand, Dee?" He was standing over me now, leaning down. I could see the bottom of his white ducks and the top of his black dress shoes.

"The kids'll be laughing at you," I said without looking up at him. There was a long silence during which I chewed on my thumbnail and Ducky stood by the couch in front of me. He had a sharp crease in his white pants and one of his shoe laces was untied.

"What do you mean, Dee?"

I looked up at him now. A frown creased his forehead as he struggled to understand.

"What are you talking about?" He asked again and then his face cleared and his lips formed a bewildered involuntary "Oh" as realization set in.

"Dee?" He was closer, now kneeling on one knee, looking up into my face. I tried to turn away. "Dee, you didn't tell anybody I was supposed to do it to Dora, did you?" I chewed on my thumbnail and tried to close him out of my mind.

"Answer me, Dee."

My voice sounded strange even to my own ears, and I cleared my throat trying to talk around the knot. "They don't have to know, Ducky," I said.

He dropped down on the floor, his chin resting on one knee. I placed my hand on his arm and he immediately jerked it away.

"I don't believe you did that," he said, shaking his head slowly. "I just can't believe it."

I suddenly remembered Deborah Kerr in *Tea and Sympathy* and for one wild second I thought of grabbing his hand and taking him upstairs to prove to him and to myself that he wasn't "funny," but I knew it wouldn't have worked if nobody else knew and I couldn't bear to have the other kids know, especially James Albert.

"Ducky, I... "

"Dee, James Albert?" I heard the front door open and soon after my mother appeared under the light in the front hall. I heard a click and light flooded the livingroom.

"How come it's so dark in here?" She eyed Ducky suspiciously.

"Hi, Mom," I said.

Ducky edged towards the door. "Well, see you later, Dee. Goodnight Mrs. King."

"Ducky, wait a minute... " I headed towards the door behind him.

"Just where do you think you're going?" my mother said, her hands on her hips.

"Mom, please, I'm not going off the block," I begged. Something in my manner must have indicated how important this was to me because she held firm for a moment and then relented, pointing to the clock on the mantle-piece. "Make sure you're back here in ten minutes, girl."

By the time I got to the steps, he was already stepping past his grandmother to get into the house. I came back inside and called him, letting the phone ring fifteen times. But when his mother answered, I just hung up.

I suppose my betrayal was the last straw because Ducky finally gave up on trying to be accepted on Beechwood Street. He stopped speaking to most of us, especially to me, and started hanging out with some of the kids from the Catholic school he attended. If I saw him on the street, he would cross over to the other side to avoid me. Although that marked the end of our friendship, eventually he would respond to my hello. Later he would stop and make small talk with me.

"How you doing?" I'd ask.

"Fine."

"You still playing the violin?"

"Uh huh."

"I won first place in a poetry contest at school."

"That's great, Dee." And I could tell he was sincere, but, eventually, he would remember something he had to do and hurry off. He never came back over to my house and we never again discussed the incident about Dora Johnson. And although I wanted to make up, wanted to approach him again to make an effort to mend our relationship, I never did. I was cowed by the thought of going to him and being rejected, so I was trying to make some space between the zenith of his anger and my attempt at reconciliation.

I must have waited too long though, because soon my family moved again, this time into an apartment in the new high-rise across Diamond Street about nine blocks from Beechwood Street. I thought many times about going back over and trying to talk with Ducky, but, pursued by my guilt and cowardice, I finally convinced myself that maybe it would be better if I just left it alone. Then I heard from one of my brother's friends that Ducky and his mom had moved back to Connecticut again and it was too late.

Although I don't think Ducky was gay when we were fifteen and best friends, and I'm not one to ask how a person becomes gay anymore than I'd ask why some women like tall men or older men, I still can't help wondering what effect the events of that last summer had on Ducky's coming out eventually as a gay man. I don't know exactly when he came out or what changes he might have gone through in the process. I heard he'd come out about ten years after we moved from Beechwood Street. I heard it through the grapevine. Or, more explicitly, my brother told me. I was twenty-three at the time, pregnant with Denise and separated from my first husband. I had returned to Philadephia to stay with my brother who had married Shirley and bought a house in West Philadelphia. (Dora Johnson eventually became the celibate minister of a storefront church on Dauphin Street.)

One morning he came home from the post office where he worked third shift and said to me before he'd even kissed Shirley hello, "Hey, Dee, guess who's a faggot?"

"Who?"

"What'sisname? That sissified dude that used to hang out at our house all the time when we lived on Beechwood Street. What'sisname? You know, Dee!"

"Ducky?"

"Yeah, him. Lionel saw him walking down the street with this real swish, looking like he could just eat him up."

"That doesn't mean Ducky's that way."

"They were standing in front of a gay bar."

"That still doesn't mean Ducky's that way. The other guy, maybe, but not Ducky. And how did Lionel know it was a gay bar?"

"Lionel's a cabbie!"

"Well, I still don't believe it."

"Suit yourself." He shrugged his shoulders and leaned down and kissed his wife.

About a year ago, after my second marriage broke up in D.C. and I returned with Denise to Philadelphia to live, I tried to find Ducky again. I went through the telephone book and called every McPhearson listed and when I found Ducky's grandmother, I asked her how I could get in touch with him. She told me that Ducky's mother had recently remarried and bought a home in a "nice" neighborhood in a Philadelphia suburb, and that Ducky had returned to live with her while majoring in music at Temple. He now lived in New York where he had a job as music director at a small private school. She gave me his address and telephone number and I take it with me each time I go to New York to see my agent, but so far I have put off contacting him.

I'd like to think that if Ducky is gay, and I suspect now that he is, that he isn't leading a double life, that he hasn't succumbed to the pressure of getting married and having 2.3 kids with a station wagon and wife in the suburbs. I'd like to think that he's maintained his personal integrity enough so that he isn't one of those guys who go to gay bars straight from work, still dressed in their "nine-to-five-clothes" to make a pick-up before going home to some poor wife who thinks it's her fault that her husband is unhappy. And I'd like to think that, maybe, someday, even after all these years, that Ducky and I have enough in common to want to share things together: to listen to Issac Stern or old fifties records, or take Denise and Timmie's seats at the chessboard and discuss and finally bury the ghost of the betrayal that estranged us when we were kids on Beechwood Street in North Philly.

Symbols

"Do you have to wear that?" He was walking down Walnut Street without looking at her. His hands were in his pockets and he was staring down at his spit-shined brown shoes.

"Do I have to wear what?"

He looked over at her now. She wore a short Afro and large hoop earrings that brushed her neck when she turned to look at him.

"Do you have to wear that thing around your neck?" he said. They were on their way to a play he'd already seen months before. The tickets were a Father's Day gift from his brother, Arthur. They had come inside a white envelope and were hand-delivered by a thin woman with ultra long, flame red fingernails. She was supposed to have been his blind date. This had also been arranged by his brother. On the way home from seeing the play the first time the woman had casually dropped her hand into his lap. He wasn't interested though. He was afraid he'd catch some disease that he would take back to Dee, the woman walking beside him now.

It was late afternoon and sweltering. As Barry and Dee walked toward the theater, Barry carried his beige jacket draped across his arm because he expected the theater to be air-conditioned and also because this was a special occasion: the first time they'd had dinner together after a six-month separation. He was disappointed that she had shown up in jeans and a short-sleeved Danskin but he refused to accept this as a negative omen. He had picked her up a couple hours earlier and they had dined in the quiet restaurant with the hanging chandeliers. It was the same place he had taken her to celebrate their eighth year together. The other celebration had represented their third year of marriage. They had lived together five years before his divorce from his first wife became final. His ex-wife got the house, the second car and a third of his salary until Joshua, then six, and Elizabeth, then seven, turned eighteen. He got the right to marry Dee and introduce her to his kids.

He'd seen her a total of six times since he reluctantly moved out of their apartment, four times when he'd returned on the pretext of picking up some clothes. Once she'd called him about two a.m. because she'd lost the keys to her motorcycle in Fairmount Park. He'd gotten out of bed at half past two, driven around in the semi-darkness until he'd found her, then he'd driven her home to pick up her extra set of keys. He had waited there with his motor running until she'd kick-started the bike and then he sat watching the red and amber taillight and the reflection of her helmet moving down Kelly Drive. Then he'd put his Chrysler into gear and headed for home. He noticed that she had appeared depressed and anxious but she had allowed him to hold her hand in the car. He had driven back to his parents' house wondering whether or not that was significant.

At the restaurant earlier today, he had not become upset when Dee insisted on splitting the bill. He found the idea amusing, as if this were their first date and she had to make sure she didn't owe him anything, wouldn't have to go to bed with him afterwards. Still, he knew better than to laugh. He could be liberal if he had to, but mostly he was just satisfied to be spending time with her again.

When he picked her up for their date he had already angered her by inadvertently extending the boundaries of their agreement for seeing each other. As he stepped inside the apartment she embraced him, and when their pelvises touched it ignited a spontaneous bolt of electricity that coursed through his groin and he had been unable to suppress a groan. She had pulled away embarrassed and he'd had to listen to the ground rules of their relationship again. Friendship. They got past that once he explained to her quite truthfully that he was just happy spending time with her again. He had not added that friendship was acceptable only if that was all that was offered.

Everything was fine until he noticed the thing around her neck. Even after he'd first seen it he walked several blocks distracted in his conversation, trying not to say anything. But then she looked over at him with his hands in his pockets and asked, "What's the matter?"

He said, "Nothing."

And she said, "You know I can always tell when something's bothering you." It was then that he'd asked if she had to wear that thing.

She reached up and grabbed her double women's symbol as if it was so much a part of herself she could find it at night in a room totally devoid of light, as she might find her arm. "This?" she asked.

"Yeah," he nodded his head and looked away at passengers erupting out of a bus at the corner of 16th and Locust Streets. "That's a lesbian symbol, isn't it?"

"Why, yes," she said, a trace of irritation (or was it defiance?) in her voice. They stared at each other in separate pools of silence.

"Does it bother you?" she asked finally.

"Well, yeah. . . " This was no time to lie. He started to say something else but stopped himself.

"Why?"

"Huh?"

"Why does it bother you?" She stopped walking and stared him in the face, trying to hold his gaze, but he looked away—down at his shoes, at the bus about to pull away from the curb.

It bothers me because I love you. Because I need you to want me the way I still want you. Because the symbol suggests you never will.

"I don't know, it just does," he said aloud.

"And you want me to take it off?"

"I don't want to fight about it, Dee." He touched her elbow and nudged her forward.

She allowed herself to be led a few steps, then balked. If there was one thing he could not stand, it was a public scene.

"Look, this is what I am, Barry. I wear it with a degree of pride, alright? Asking me to take it off would be like asking me to take down my freedom flag." He pictured the red, green and black freedom flags that were sewn on the pockets of her work suits. The ones she wore as a gym teacher.

"Dee, I know you're a lesbian," he said softly. From the corner of his eye he peeped at the passing dyads and, leaning closer, said "lesbian" without moving his lips, as if he didn't want anyone to hear the word "lesbian" coming from his mouth. "I know you're a lesbian," he repeated with the same strained effort, "but you're with me now."

"I'm lesbian wherever I go, and this goes wherever I go." She held it out in front of her as if it were an amulet warding off evil spirits.

He sighed deeply and moved his jacket to his other arm. Telling her to be quiet now, he decided, would be the worst thing he could do. Changing the subject wouldn't work either. When Dee was being self-righteous there was no hushing her up. Once during an argument he'd made the mistake of asking her to be quiet so the neighbors would not hear and Dee started yelling at the top of her voice while he ran around the apartment furiously pulling down the windows. The memory brought a frown to his face.

A tall, blond man in horn-rimmed glasses bumped into Barry and Barry stepped back and apologized. He moved to the side of Anthony's Pizza Parlor where Dee was leaning against the wall, one foot propped up behind her. She was still holding the women's symbol, cradling it protectively, her hand resting against her orange Danskin. She wore a button pinned to her shoulder bag with "Hera" stamped on it. Hera was the name of the women's bookstore where Dee did volunteer work. Actually it was a lesbian bookstore but he didn't like to think about that. He didn't like to think of Dee referring to herself as lesbian at all. Thoughts like that confounded and depressed him, creating questions about their relationship he hadn't the courage to face.

He looked across Walnut Street at a block-long line of people waiting to see *Star Wars*. A patrol car was passing slowly, the officer inside watching Dee, an "Is he bothering you miss?" expression on his face.

"Why don't we just forget about the play." She sounded as tired as he felt.

"And waste forty dollars!" He took her elbow and

nudged her forward then felt the weight of her resistance and stopped again. Depression engulfed him like a wet cloud. When he turned to face her again she had both hands on her hips and she was frowning. He sucked his teeth and leaned back against the wall, his hands in his pockets. This was not supposed to be happening. He was ready to just give up, give Dee the tickets and go on home alone. Only Dee wouldn't accept the tickets.

"Why do you always manage to make me feel guilty?" she asked.

"I'm not trying to make you feel guilty," he said, "I just don't want to see the play anymore."

"Maybe it's too early for us to try to spend time together," Dee said.

"Or maybe it's too late," Barry mumbled. He held no hope of salvaging the evening.

"Huh?"

"Never mind," he said, "I'll take you home."

II

Later in his apartment, with his feet on the coffee table and a beer in his hand, Barry wondered how Dee could suddenly decide at twenty-nine that she liked women better than men. Shouldn't there have been some clues? In her adolescence? Eighteen months ago she'd told him she "thought" she might have "homosexual tendencies." She borrowed books from the library. They both borrowed books from the library. And since he had no doubt that she did love him once and perhaps loved him still, deep down, why now, in the tenth year of what she'd referred to as the best relationship she'd ever had, was she wanting to be with women?

The only other lesbian he'd known was Myrtle

McHenry, a tall thick-shouldered woman who, even in junior high school, more closely resembled a man than a woman. Once, three of the boys from Bainbridge Street had grabbed Myrtle and tried to yank her clothes off to see what she wore underneath. They succeeded but Barry wondered if the razor slash that still puckers Junebug's left eyebrow had been worth finding out that Myrtle wore her breasts tied down with an ace bandage and that she donned white cotton panties under her men's pants. At any rate, Barry saw no connection between Myrtle and Dee except that Dee maintained that North Philadelphia stroll she developed as a kid growing up in the Raymond Rosen projects.

Thinking about her now he could still see a trace of the adolescent Dee. Six months in charm and modeling school had not erased her tendency to bounce like a Philly corner boy. When she wore her hair straightened and curled, and when she wore those cute little skirts and pumps she did not appear as, well, androgynous as she did now. There was a boyishness about her that her voluptuous ass could not deny. That was what first attracted him to her, her ass.

They met in Washington, D.C. during Ralph Abernathy's first mass civil rights demonstration after Dr. King's death. Barry had been separated from the bus he rode down on and it had taken off without him. He jumped on the bus chartered by the union from Dee's job and asked it if was going back to Philly.

"Somebody got left. Somebody got left," the voice in sing-song fashion came from a seat just behind the driver. Barry looked over at an attractive young woman in a powder-blue shell wearing a curly brown wig. He smiled but he did not think it amusing. He was embarrassed and concerned about getting back home. He turned to the woman with the teasing voice. She had full lips and a mole on the side of her face.

"Is this bus going back to Philly?"

"Yep," she replied with an impish grin.

"Can I ride with you?"

"I guess so but you'd better check with the shop steward."

Barry sat down in the seat in front of her and rode with his head craned backwards, talking with her for about forty-five minutes. Some boozed-up coworkers were singing golden oldies in the back of the bus and he was beginning to get nauseous from riding backwards. Finally, she asked him if he wouldn't be more comfortable if he sat beside her.

At a rest stop he got his first glance at her ass and, although there were other things he liked about her, it was the sight of her exiting the bus in front of him in those tight jeans that made him ask her out.

She stood him up the first time they were supposed to go out. Left him standing in front of a laundromat in South Philadelphia while a group of white teenagers on roller skates played hockey in the middle of the street. He waited an hour in his charcoal gray suit and black tie and then he went home. When he called her later from a pay phone she told him she had forgotten. Later she told the truth: she had gotten cold feet. Never before had she dated a married man.

The second time they went out he took her to a race track, partly because he liked horse racing but mostly because the race track was in New Jersey. He didn't want to have to concern himself with being seen.

Afterwards he dropped her off at an address in North Philadelphia and Dee would later tease him about going home horny while she made love with her ex-boyfriend. She said he shouldn't have been jealous because he went home each night to his wife. He had tried repeatedly to explain that he hadn't slept with his wife in a very long time. Sometimes Dee believed this and sometimes she didn't, but it was more or less true. For the year before he met Dee he had rarely slept with his wife. Sometimes he just went into the bedroom with a "you're my wife... " attitude. But it was rarely worth the effort to make love with a woman who just laid there and waited until it was over. Even at that he was afraid of getting her pregnant. They already had two children and a marriage that was obviously finished.

In contrast, he and Dee had had an almost idyllic relationship. He didn't believe it when she said she was attracted to women. It had surprised him when she started going to the lesbian community center. Next had come the volunteer work at Hera, then the consciousness-raising group followed promptly by a slew of "dates." He had withstood the casual flings much better than he had endured the first weekend she spent out of town.

That Sunday he read the sports page, did the *New York Times* crossword puzzle and she still hadn't come home. She called from the train station but there was time only for "hello" and "got here safely" and reassurances that she would be back in time to go to dinner with him Sunday evening. Then the phone went dead and he imagined she was walking towards a cab, her lover carrying her bags. It was already half past two and he wanted to get out of the house, walk over to Hank's, or maybe drive over to his parents' house to see if the kids were visiting. Mostly he just wanted to get out of the house to make the waiting easier. Since ten that morning he had been preparing for her arrival, straightening up the living room, fielding questions from family and friends. "She didn't tell me she had a friend in New York," her Aunt Bertha had said. It was the absurdity of it all that prompted him to call her at her lover's apartment. Why was he sitting home acting like her secretary while she carried out her long distance affair?

He was sitting on the couch, the T.V. tuned to a talk show featuring some politicians all dressed in suits of varying shades of gray. They were debating something Barry could not hear because the volume was turned all the way down. The radio was on, tuned to "Amazon Country," the local women's radio station. Dee had discovered it from a newspaper she picked up at the lesbian center. On Sunday afternoon he and Dee usually listened to that station and, although he now thought of changing the station to some music, he sat leaning over the coffee table staring, eyes unfocused, at a book on the aerospace industry. He was supposed to be studying for a test for a promotion at his job in the accounting department in city hall. He thought about Dee's journal/telephone book on the nightstand next to her side of the bed.

He stood up then and, as he leaned over to switch the dial, his jealousy aroused, he thought suppose she didn't go to New York to see a woman. Suppose she went to see a man? The thought of Dee impaled beneath a naked, sweating man filled him with such despair he immediately sank back down under the weight of it. It had brought back memories of his ex-wife, Jeannie and her "cousin from Georgia." One hot August night when he'd come home early from his Friday night poker game, he had seen what he thought was his wife getting into a car with Georgia license plates. It had been dark, the street poorly lit and he'd been almost half a block away. He called out her name, then chased behind the car running hard the way they taught him in track. He'd been gaining on the red tail-lights too until the car suddenly sped up and he stopped, exhausted. It had looked like his wife, in the car, the height was the same, she wore the same curly bush. But later, in their bedroom, he in his jockey shorts and she in her yellow nightie, the door closed so the kids couldn't hear them, she'd denied it all.

The more he obsessed about it, the more he convinced himself that the only reasonable course of action was to call Dee at her lover's apartment.

"Hello," the husky voice on the other end sounded almost like Dee when just awakened. Why was she asleep at two in the afternoon?

"Hello," he said tentatively, then more confidently, "May I speak to Dee Spicer please?"

"Who is this?" the voice asked suspiciously.

"Barry—Barry Spicer," he said struggling to keep his voice calm and free of hostility. Had they been making love? "May I speak to my wife please?"

There was a loud clatter that hurt his ears, the phone being dropped.

"Why did you give that man my number? I don't play that shit!" The voice coming through the dropped receiver, crisp, angry.

"I didn't give him your number." Dee now, annoyed and defensive.

He could deal with Dee's anger, but a more horrid fear took away his breath. What if Dee refused to come to the phone? What if they hung up on him? He realized now that the question of male or female was trivial. It would be no less painful if she were with a man.

"Hello," Dee was on the phone now, her voice guarded.

He breathed a sigh of relief and then his mind went blank ". . . uh Dee?"

"Why did you call me here, Barry?" She sounded unconcerned. Suppose he was sick? Suppose he needed her to sign him in or out of a hospital? He was angry then as if he were actually in a hospital and his wife responded as if she were more concerned about appeasing her girlfriend.

"Where did you get this number, Barry?"

"I got it out of your telephone book."

A voice in the background, the girlfriend, "Hang up the phone."

"Barry, you shouldn't have called me here."

He heard the intrusive voice again, "Hang up the phone. You can't talk to your man on my damn phone."

"Tell that bitch to shut up," Barry said.

Both voices through the receiver, muffled conversation he could not decipher.

Dee back on the line again. "Is everything alright there?" she asked.

"Yeah, you coming home soon?"

"I'll be catching the five forty-five."

"I'll meet you at the station, okay?"

"Sure. . . you really shouldn't have called me here."

"I miss you," he said.

"We'll talk about it," she said and hung up.

They talked about it three months later on the tennis court. It was like old times; an impromptu picnic on a lazy Sunday morning, a six-pack of beer, potato salad, fried chicken and barbecue from a rib joint on South Street.

The difference in their relationship was reflected in Dee's tennis game. She had always been a fierce competitor. She hated to lose almost as much as Barry did and would play any ball at which she had the remotest chance. He liked that about her. But that day she hit the ball tentatively. Even the suggestion that she was letting him win was not sufficient to prevent her lackluster taps across the net or her flailing helplessly at balls that the old Dee would have chased down at top speed. When Barry won the last set, Dee broke down and cried right there on the tennis court. He was embarrassed. Not knowing what else to do he put his arms around her and walked her off the court.

"Why are you crying?" he asked her.

"I don't know, I'm just so unhappy." She dabbed at her eyes with a napkin but the tears kept flowing. She was sitting on a picnic table, her tennis racket lying across her lap.

Dee had broken up with the woman from New York. He didn't fool himself into thinking that it had anything to do with him. The bottom line was that even though she went to Gay Activists Alliance meetings on Monday nights, the Lesbian Center on Saturdays, Club Olympia, a Black Gay/Lesbian club once a week, Dee came home to sleep every night. He thought things were returning to normal. It shocked him to hear of her acute unhappiness.

"I'm sorry I'm making you unhappy," she said.

"I can take care of myself," he said. He had been afraid she would bring up the subject of breaking up again. The last time they discussed his unhappiness was that Sunday evening three months ago after she had returned from New York. Afterwards they had split all the bills and divided up all the housework. At least in theory they were roommates.

Barry looked with envy at a couple in identical white

short sets who were kissing at the net. He grabbed another napkin and helped Dee dab at her eyes too.

"Maybe you ought to talk to somebody... " he said. He was afraid of offending her and said the words softly so she could not hear him if she didn't want to, "... like a therapist or something? I mean," he rambled on, "I mean it wouldn't imply there's anything wrong with you or anything." He shrugged his shoulders. "I saw one myself right after I got out of the Marines." She squirmed in his arms as if he was holding her too tightly and he released her. For the first time he allowed himself to consider the possibility that she might feel smothered.

"Maybe I should just move out for a while," he said, "Give you a chance to decide what you really want to do?"

As a last effort to salvage his marriage he moved out of the apartment and returned to his parents' house. It was intended as a temporary move.

He had been out of the house a month when Dee agreed to see the shrink. Twice they both went to see a young white woman with long hair and sandals who told Dee she wasn't really a lesbian, but that she just wasn't dealing with some resentment she had against her father.

They both went back to the library for more books. He became drawn to the ones on bisexuality and began to think of her in those terms. He lowered his expectations. It occurred to him that they could go on like this forever: Dee going to gay bars and gay activist meetings a couple days per week, and being Mrs. Barry Spicer the rest of the week. It worked with other couples, why not with them? He had called her up, invited her to dinner and a play to talk about it.

III

The next weekend Barry sat with Arthur in the living room of their parents' house with the still-unused theater tickets in his pocket. He had inadvertently pulled them out when he reached into his jacket pocket at the Garden State Race Track.

"Do you notice how Dee walks sometimes, man, the way she bounces when she walks?" Barry asked.

"Yeah, man," Arthur said casually chewing on his pipe stem. They were waiting until their father returned from the circus with the two sets of kids. Arthur's wife, Helene, was visiting her relatives in South Jersey.

"I don't think Dee and I are getting back together, man."

"You like Donna's cousin, Terry?" Arthur's eyes brightened, which irritated Barry. Arthur never liked Dee. Terry was the thin one with the red fingernails, the woman Arthur once fixed Barry up with. She didn't know who George Jackson was and saw no reason Ray Charles should not perform in South Africa. And her nails were too long. She was not Dee. "It doesn't have anything to do with Terry, it's just about Dee and me," Barry said.

"No problem," Arthur said. He sat watching while Barry drummed his fingers on the end table.

"What's the longest time you've ever been separated from a woman and still got back together with her?"

"About a year and a half. I used to go with this bisexual who came to me to get tuned up between affairs with women. She was a neat lady," he said with some regret. They were both silent for a moment, then Arthur said, "But, you know if a woman likes chocolate ice cream she ain't gonna settle for vanilla for too long." He relit his pipe and studied Barry's face.

"But wouldn't they rather have both if they could?" Barry said.

"Maybe. But you can't have both, man. Not for long."

He met Dee's new girlfriend when he went to get the rest of his clothes. When he saw her in the hall he knew immediately who she was. Partly it was his sixth sense, but mostly it was because she wore a lavender T-shirt that had "Killer Dyke" silk-screened on the front in large silver letters. She had passed him on the second landing. He found her standing in the kitchen when he let himself in with his key. Dee was standing at the stove frying steak. Dee too, had on one of those absurd lavender T-shirts, only hers read "Sappho" on the front.

"I think I passed you in the hall," the girlfriend said, holding out her hand and smiling the smile of a current lover who could afford to be gracious.

"Pleased to meet you." He could play the polite game too. Well, at least the girlfriend wasn't offering tea as if she had already moved in. He shook her hand. It was soft. Much softer than Dee's. Dee's lover had no ass but she had firm breasts that sat up under her shirt. She wore no bra. There would be no mistaking her for a boy. She was soft, petite and feminine and he could have forgiven her everything except the "Killer Dyke" T-shirt. If they walked down the street like that—advertising—everybody would know. Suppose his parents saw them? Or his kids? Except for Dee's earrings and her breasts, which were smaller than her girlfriend's, she might easily have been mistaken for a teenaged boy. The idea revolted him and he frowned involuntarily. He disliked lesbians now. All of them.

He walked into the bedroom closet and pulled out two suitcases Dee had already packed. On the way out he stopped in the kitchen again, curious. Dee was chopping cucumbers for a salad. The girlfriend sat at the table reading to Dee from what appeared to be a poetry book. He put the suitcases back into the closet. He would get them another time when he would not have to walk past Dee's lover to get them out.

He motioned to Dee from the kitchen doorway. "Can I speak to you, Dee?" Dee looked up at him then over at her lover. She rinsed her hands at the sink and followed him out into the hallway.

"You're in love with her, huh?"

Dee nodded her head.

"I guess this is it." He handed her the key and stood there as if he couldn't decide what he should do next.

"Maybe in a few months we can talk some more?" Dee said.

"I wouldn't bet the mortgage on that," he said. But he smiled when he said it. Almost as an afterthought, he threw her an air kiss. And then he walked out closing the door softly behind him.

Outside it had begun to rain, but he didn't want to go back inside the apartment to get his umbrella. He walked past his car parked across the street, then stopped and looked up at the apartment window. Dee was at the sink washing dishes. He rolled his collar up and continued walking towards Center City. He decided to call Terry. Maybe he could get her to cut those damn fingernails.

OPHELIA

Ophelia McNeil Kennedy wanted me to go with her to the jazz festival in Atlantic City. She leaned over the side of my chair, rubbed my stomach and made wild, passionate pleas to my sense of Black culture. I sat leafing through an old issue of *Lesbian Connection,* ignoring her as best I could ignore someone who set fireflies zipping through my blood. I like jazz but most of the instrumentalists headlining the show at the Civic Center left me cold. Besides, I had already made plans to do something else with a friend.

When all else failed, Ophelia appealed to my sense of ethnic pride. "You'd really rather go hear your White girlfriend read poetry than listen to the brothers jam?"

"Yes," I said, refusing to take the bait. Ophelia wore the mischievous smile she reserved for implying my relationships with White women made my Black consciousness suspect. Ophelia and I had been lovers for six months and had an open relationship which allowed space for sex with others—though the option didn't have to be explored. Ophelia preferred to keep her affairs private, booking no "where you been where you going?" questions. I felt sharing information made the difference between an open relationship and plain old slipping around corners. Ophelia won that argument, however, because

67

she wore her "I'm a private person" statements like a shield. I evened the score by not correcting her when she implied that I was sleeping with all the women I spent time with.

The friend I planned to see this night, Susan, was a heterosexual psychologist from my writers' support group who thought Ophelia's elevator didn't go all the way to the twelfth floor. I disputed this loudly and often but did not bother sharing this assessment with Ophelia. If I had planned to spend time with my friend Wydia, Ophelia would not only have approved, she would have wanted to tag along.

"I cannot believe Miss Karen here is actually going to pass up the brothers for this White girl. I just cannot believe it."

I smiled and kept browsing through my magazine. I was sitting in a lounge chair in Ophelia's backyard, which was fairly private except for the second floor patio on the condo across the street. Ophelia was sitting on the grass beside me, arms across my lap, her auburn hair splayed across my designer jeans. Her hand was resting provocatively on the inside of my thigh. Out of the corner of my eye I caught movement on the patio across the way. I pointed out to Ophelia that the retired dentist who had complained to the police about the volume of the Zodiac benefit two months ago was standing on the patio again. She dismissed this with a wave of her hand.

"I don't give a good damn about that middle-class motherfucker," she said with a giggle. Ophelia enjoyed thumbing her nose at the White neighbors who inhabited her well-integrated neighborhood. She thought of this as an indication of her commitment to her inner self. Ophelia's inner self was Black.

Before the man could leave the patio Ophelia started in

on me again, always with a good natured smile. I tolerated Ophelia's frequent bouts of "I know what's best for you" teasing because it was always done with good humor. Ophelia never failed to see the ridiculous in any situation, and had no problem laughing. And although she took herself very seriously she might have laughed loudest at herself.

"You're just not going to the jazz festival because you've got a case of the Black ass," she said. "That's the real reason you're not going, Miss Karen."

"I've already committed myself to go to this reading," I said patiently. Ophelia took a sip of the wine she drank from a long-stemmed glass and laid that slow, sexy smile on me.

"That chick must have some good pussy," she said, her smile still in place. I blushed and went back behind my magazine. "Is that it, Miss Karen, the White girl got good pussy?" She rubbed my stomach again. "I tell you, Miss Karen, I don't know what I'm going to do with your liberal Black ass!"

Ophelia found references to Black anatomy parts endearing. Once when she told me to kiss her Black ass, I promptly informed her that in the section of North Philly where I grew up, "kiss my ass" on any pretext was fighting words. Even when said with a smile. I could have short-circuited the entire conversation by pointing out that Ophelia McNeil Kennedy was a White girl, but that would have violated the unspoken terms upon which my relationship with Ophelia existed. To love Ophelia you had to accept her inner self.

"Well, if you gotta go to this stupid reading to hear some silly White girl brag about her hairy armpits, then go right ahead. But I'm certainly disappointed."

Ophelia had clear, rigid ideas about how working-class

Black folks operated. I was expected to live up to those expectations lest I reveal a middle-class mentality.

Ophelia moved into my lap on the chaise lounge and ran her fingers across my short Afro. I felt the tip of her tongue in my mouth. The warmth spread down into my abdomen. Reluctantly, I pulled my head away. "I gotta go, Ophelia. More important, I want to go." I'd stopped trying to read the magazine and hadn't protested when she took it out of my hand. She got off my lap and I glanced across the street in time to see the skinny dentist with his caved-in chest walking off the patio. He had a white beach towel around his waist.

"Maybe Pookie will go with me," Ophelia teased. Pookie was the six-foot Amazon Ophelia had broken up with several years ago. Though neither had attended college, Ophelia and Pookie wrote grants that funded a shelter for battered women. Ophelia still ran the successful business, with an all-Black staff, of course. Pookie, who grew up on Columbia Avenue, now made close to forty thousand a year as security consultant for a large department store chain. Pookie had lived with Ophelia for eight years, and set the criteria for what was Black enough and what was too bourgeois.

"Sounds like a good idea to me," I said. When you're in a non-monogamous relationship you can't appear jealous. I learned that the hard way from the first woman I loved. She was a former Flower Child who came to the women's movement through the peace movement.

"You don't care if I go out with Pookie?"

"Hey, you gotta love with open hands." I smiled and winked at her. "Isn't that what Pookie Brown would say?"

. . .

The first time I met Ophelia was at a Zodiac fundraiser. The event was held in Ophelia's backyard and was limited to Black women only. The only exceptions were Ophelia and a faintly effeminate Black gay man who was a cousin of Blanche's, the Zodiac president. Zodiac was the name of the social and, to a much lesser extent, political group of which Ophelia was co-coordinator. My oldest lesbian friend, Florence, and I attended the formal affair in rented white tuxedos.

When I first saw Ophelia, she was opening the door for us in a black satin dress with white trim. She had this effervescent smile that lit up her plain face and, without knowing why, I was hooked. From the time Florence introduced us, Ophelia and I bumped heads in the manner perfected by people who are attracted to each other but cannot figure out why. I couldn't piece together why a bright, articulate White woman who appeared not only self-confident but downright cocky socialized in exclusively Black circles. Ophelia, who left the women's movement charging racism and classism in the early '70s, couldn't make sense of a working-class Black woman with good self-esteem who was still hanging out with middle-class White feminists who "ate Black women up then spat them out," to quote her.

We were not polite. "You're just playing Queen Bee," I said. "You've got Blanche and all these apolitical Black women fawning over you, so you're as happy as a tick in a blood bank. You can't stand competition from other White women. Your life is an urban Tarzan movie with you as b'wanna, Ophelia."

"First, I take exception to your insult to my friends who you don't know a damn thing about." Her hands were on her hips and her head was snapping like the Black woman she wished she was. "And secondly, most White women

couldn't stand the pressure. You think I got it easy? I pay
my dues, baby! I got to deal with hostility from Black
women like you," she said, softly tapping her slender finger in my chest, "who want to scratch my eyes out before
they take the time to find out what I'm about; and White
men who want to kick my ass 'cause they can't get in my
drawers. And I don't even want to mention those White
feminists! But I tell you what," she said, planting her
hands back on her hips, that bright smile on her face, "I
can deal with it. This White girl can stand the heat in the
kitchen 'cause Black folks are worth it!"

Florence and about thirty other women from Zodiac
danced in the living room and lounged in the backyard
while Ophelia and I sat on the front porch yelling at each
other over loud music coming from the big speakers in the
basement. She took my number and said she'd call, but
didn't. I took a Zodiac business card; I didn't call her either.

The next time I ran into Ophelia was about a month
later at a NOW conference. Ophelia was there as a vendor
selling T-shirts for Zodiac. She was also handing out flyers
with information about the battered women's shelter. I,
who hadn't been to a women's conference in over six
years, was on assignment, writing an article for a
Washington-based feminist newspaper. When I saw her
standing near the entrance to the Third World Women's
Caucus, it was curiosity more than anything else that com-
pelled me to walk up to her. I couldn't figure out why she
appeared happy to see me since I had no problem telling
her exactly how I felt about her. I expected her to tell me
to go fuck myself, or to cry like some typical middle-class
White women who have trouble dealing with Black anger
and their White guilt.

"Hi, sister," she said with that big smile followed by a

giggle. Ophelia's laughter, I later learned, was often a clue that she was feeling insecure. "How come you're not in there?" she said, nodding her head in the direction of the Third World Caucus. "Here I'd give my right arm to be in there and you got your ass somewhere else."

"Conflicts," I said, returning her smile. "They keep jamming issues important to Third World women into the same time slots."

"That's the way those White feminists are, babe." She held out both hands by her waist, palms up, to be slapped. "Pookie and I tried to point that out for years." I obligingly slapped her palms.

"I just walked out of a classism workshop. I stood it as long as I could," she giggled, "then I walked."

"I was checking out the one on incest survivors," I said. In the awkward silence that often follows the mention of incest, I checked out Ophelia's tight black leather pants and her six-inch red stack heels.

"You see anything wrong with my get up? I mean as a feminist," she said sarcastically. She turned to model for me, pointing to her white silk blouse. "Those middle-class White girls who think real lesbians are only supposed to wear jeans and sneakers piss me off." She must have noticed my faded jeans and my Adidas then because her hands flew up to her mouth. "Oops, I'm not busting on you sister, but I resent the middle-class White girl assumption that any woman who dresses up like a woman is femme. They can just kiss my Black ass!" she said and giggled again.

"You look fine to me," I said politely. I surreptitiously peeked out the corner of my eye to see if there was anyone in the hall to overhear this White woman refer to her "Black ass." There wasn't.

"The workshop on coalition building was a good one,"

I said, remembering that I'd learned to love my lesbian self through fighting homophobia in the women's movement with feminists, many of them White. "They really are trying," I said in response to Ophelia's look of skepticism.

"Trying shit!" Ophelia was warmed up now. She wore this bright red glossy lipstick which made her lips look luscious. Generally I hated women in lipstick, but I was suddenly aware of wanting to kiss her. "I am up to here," Ophelia said, pointing to a vein in her neck, "with White women who think they can change the world without dealing with their own racism and classism."

"Hey, I'll buy that." This time it was I who held out my hands to be slapped.

Ophelia stared at me like a student who has solved a difficult problem and wasn't certain how she did it.

"What's your sign?" she asked.

"Scorpio."

"A Scorpio, uh ooh!" She cocked her head flirtatiously to the side, "I'm scared of that!" She put her left hand on my shoulder and laughed as if she'd heard something uproariously funny.

We stood in the hallway talking about our stints in the women's movement as ex-G.I.s might discuss the Army. We talked about Pookie's and Ophelia's experiences—they met through the women's movement and left it together. I talked about the sometimes painful differences between working against homophobia, which my lesbian feminist sisters and I all recognized as the Goliath it was and were all willing to surround and attack as a group, and the loneliness of confronting some of the subtler forms of racism that you were embarrassed to find in someone you had grown to love like a sister.

Ophelia and I left the conference together. We drove out

to West River Drive and sat in my two-year-old red Toyota, watching the moon's reflection on the Schuylkill River. I sat behind the wheel listening to Ophelia tell me about her life. Watched her leaning against the door on the passenger side facing me, her legs folded in the lotus position, touching my hand and arm as she spoke. Those deep brown doe eyes stared into mine. Ophelia said, "I want you to get to know the 'real me'." I wanted to get to know the real Ophelia too.

Around midnight a white-haired police officer shone his spotlight into the car and, feeling like teenagers with no place to go, we moved on. We went to Ophelia's where she took off her red stack heels and I removed my Adidas.

She lit a long, white tapered candle and placed it on the nightstand by her four-poster queen-sized bed. Fully clothed, we stretched out across the pink flowered comforter and lay on our backs, our arms around each other.

Five minutes later I kissed those luscious lips for the first time and she wiggled out of her black leather pants. I removed my faded jeans and my "fesbian leminist" T-shirt and moaned as she pulled one of my nipples into her mouth.

Sometime later Ophelia reached beneath the mattress and pulled out the first dildo I had ever seen. It was the color of burnt chocolate.

"You should think of this as an extension of your hand," she said. I did.

I watched her touching my hand in the light of the flickering candle, guiding the hand that held the dildo until it entered her.

"This is your hand," she whispered. "Think of it as your hand moving in and out of me." As my hand, the dildo and Ophelia's hips all moved rhythmically towards

Ophelia's explosive orgasm, Ophelia yelled, "Fuck me, Karen, harder! Is that the best you can do?" she taunted. "Fuck my Black ass."

"You talk formal," Ophelia said. It was a little after noon and we were sitting on a park bench about six blocks from Ophelia's house in Powelton Village. I'd brought lunch and we were eating out of brown paper bags.

It was Friday, several days after I first made love with Ophelia and we'd talked about an open relationship. I didn't have to make my second shift stint at the post office until 3:30. "You talk formal," Ophelia repeated, after a heated discussion on radical feminism and classism in the women's movement. "You know, Diane noticed that too."

"If you're talking about the one who kept coming out to drag you in to dance, it's probably because she's jealous. She's obviously got a case on you. Besides, I'm a writer," I said, taking the remark for the criticism it was. "Words are my thing. You remind me of the kids who ostracized me for 'talking proper' when I was a student in high school."

"Now don't go getting pissed off," she said, stroking my arm solicitously. "I know you grew up in the projects and your mother was a hairdresser, but you been hanging out with White girls a long time and I cannot deal with middle-class women even if they happen to be Black."

I stared at her, incredulous. "I don't believe this dumb shit." I balled up my waxed paper and threw it into the trash receptacle next to the bench. A half smile twinkled at the edges of my mouth. She had to be kidding, right?

"Well, I've been thinking," she said studying her fingernails. She wasn't kidding. "I know you drive a truck for the post office, but you never contributed to your family's

income. Never had a part-time job or anything like that?"
I returned her steady stare. She pulled her eyes away.
". . . So I was concerned that maybe you had a middle-
class mentality." I continued staring, my "are you
crazy?" expression firmly planted on my face. She looked
up at me again now. "Well, we've got to get this settled,"
she said, a faint hint of annoyance showing.

"Ophelia," I said slowly, "we all gotta do what we
gotta do, and if you feel we can't have a relationship because of what you perceive as my middle-class mentality. . . " I shrugged my shoulders and took another bite of
my cheese, tomato and alfalfa sprout sandwich.

I sat for a few more minutes then got up and repacked
my things together, being careful to leave the rest of her
food. I was walking towards the car when she called to
me.

"And while we're at it," she said, pushing now, "there
is also the issue of the Phillies."

I stopped and turned towards her. "What's that?" I said
evenly. A brother who worked for the electric company
had given me five tickets to a Phillies playoff game. I
didn't particularly like baseball but Florence did, and I was
going with her, a gay brother and another lesbian couple I
owed an invitation to. The Phillies were a sensitive issue
with me, one Ophelia and I had gone over before.

"Well, I don't see how you can go see those racist Phillies," she said. She sat picking dry skin from around her
cuticles. I hadn't noticed the nail biting before. "Connie
Mack said he hated two things: milk and Blacks. I can't believe you've forgotten all that just because the Phillies are
in the pennant race."

"I come from a long line of baseball fans," I said.
"through the early fifties and late sixties my family's one
political statement was to pack a lunch and sit in the

bleachers at Connie Mack Stadium and root *against* the Phillies. Okay, so now my family has forgiven the Phillies. And it isn't on you to approve or disapprove of the decisions any Black person makes about the Phillies." I walked back to the car and started the engine before I remembered we'd both come to the park in my car. I stuck my head out the window. "You want a ride?" It was only six blocks to her house.

"No, I'll walk." She was feeding the pigeons when I pulled off.

After my shift that night I couldn't sleep. I took a shower, drank a Perrier, and tossed and turned on my futon until the clock on the nightstand read two a.m.

At two thirty-five Florence picked up the telephone on the third ring.

Florence was a visual artist who worked off-hours, but mostly at night. She was more likely to be awake if you called her at three a.m. than at nine a.m.

"What's the deal with Ophelia?" I asked.

"I don't know," she yawned, "what do you think?" Perhaps I had awakened her. One of the reasons I enjoyed confiding in Florence was because she listened well and seldom gave advice.

"I don't know," I said. "I've never been attracted to anyone like Ophelia before. She wants to meet my friend Wydia," I said cautiously. Meeting Wydia was the equivalent of meeting my mother. Except for a great aunt in a nursing home here, my family was based in Georgia, but Wydia represented my longest uninterrupted friendship. She was a Black separatist who thought White women were Trojan horses put here to test Black men. She fully expected Black women to be indifferent to the temptation.

"Is Wydia interested in meeting Ophelia?" asked Florence.

"Well, you know Wydia," I hedged. "Besides, it's only been a few weeks. I haven't talked to her about Ophelia yet."

I laid back on the bed and propped my feet against the wall. "Yesterday afternoon we had this stupid discussion about whether we could have a relationship despite my 'middle-class mentality.'"

"What?"

"Believe it." I said. "When Ophelia was twelve her father left and her mother went on welfare. Ophelia and her brother had to take odd jobs to help augment the family income. Since I never worked as a teenager, she suspects my thought processes work like those of upper- and middle-class White girls who never had to struggle for anything. Well, I didn't think of it at the time, but when my mother screwed up all her courage to go down to the welfare board to get help, they wouldn't let her have it. They told her to go find my father. And you want to know something else absurd? Ophelia complains that her mother used to have to charge escargot and caviar at the gourmet food section of Wanamakers because she had a charge account and they often didn't have any cash to buy food at the local store. Now, I didn't think of this until last night when I was working, but my mother couldn't afford an account at Wanamakers."

The more I thought about it, the angrier I got. "My mother got sucked into finance companies who charged an arm and a leg in interest and then sent nasty letters and made harassing phone calls until she took the rent money to get them off her back. I feel like calling her White ass right now and cussing her out."

"Well, Ophelia's had a hard life," Florence said. Another of Florence's endearing qualities was her tendency to defend women, even if they were wrong.

"Do you have any idea why she and Pookie Brown broke up?" I asked.

There was this deliberate silence which always indicated that Florence was torn between lying and saying something less than flattering about a friend. "Well, Pookie got somewhat possessive towards the end of their relationship and I heard she used to kick Ophelia's behind."

"Oh."

"If I'd been a middle-class White girl I would never have survived," Ophelia said, narrowly missing an electric blue Datsun as she swerved my car into the fast lane.

She called me a few days after that argument and we decided to go camping upstate. In another half hour we'd be at the campsite. "You know who taught me to survive?"

"Pookie Brown?"

"You damn right," Ophelia said with that intense hearty laugh. "Pookie taught me to be tough out of necessity, girlfriend. That included hassling with her to get her to pay her share of the rent, and standing in the middle of Columbia Avenue fighting her Black ass for the car when I needed it to go shopping, and she needed it to go to a fucking basketball game. And it was MY goddamned car in the first place."

"Did you and Pookie fight often?" The thought made me uneasy.

"Only when we had to. You got problems with that, Miss Karen? That's just because you been hanging out with them damn middle-class White girls too long," Ophelia said, slapping the steering wheel. "The goddess sent me here to save your Black ass. That's my goal in life,

to save Karen Howard from the White girls. Shit," she
said, soberly now, "fighting for what you believe in is just
real, baby."

"It sounds unhealthy to me," I said.

"Unhealthy! Now don't get clinical on me, Miss
Karen." She stopped talking while she checked the rear
view mirror and got into the right hand lane to exit the
turnpike onto Highway 80. When she spoke again she was
on the offensive. Ophelia had a knack for suddenly switch-
ing to the offensive, but I was willing to avoid the argument, anyway.

"You're sounding like a psychologist again. You sure
you don't have a Ph.D. stashed somewhere?"

"Now look..." I'd been riding with my hand on her
thigh. I took it off.

"I'm sorry, sugar," Ophelia drawled. "Can we call a
truce? Okay, please? I mean we just made up from our last
serious discussion," she laughed. "And I don't want your
ass mad at me again." She placed her hand on my bare
thigh. We both wore cutoff jeans and T-shirts. I nodded,
smiled and covered her hand on my thigh.

Our radio station was fading but we soon found some
semi-classical music. We rode past corn fields and cows
grazing in fields that looked far more like the familiar
country scenes of my native Georgia than Pennsylvania.

Eventually we drove through a small town and past a
yard with an old dilapidated house and rusting cars in the
front yard. A man with a straw hat sat on rotten wooden
steps drinking what looked like corn liquor from a mason
jar. I noticed three children in dirty overalls swinging on
swings fashioned from tires suspended from a rope.
Ophelia must have noticed them before we passed too because she said in a voice that sounded like her usual disdain
for White folks, "That's P.W.T."

"What's P.W.T.?" I asked.

"Poor White Trash."

"Oh," I said. Mindful of our agreement not to deal with politics, I rode on for a few more yards, staring through the windshield at a yellow Volkswagen with Michigan license plates. Then I decided I could not let that pass. "That was an extremely classist remark," I said. I made no effort to hide my annoyance.

Ophelia completed a left turn onto a gravel road and then responded, "No, it wasn't." She brushed her long hair back over her shoulder. "That's my roots, baby." Her eyes misted over. I placed my arm across the back of her seat and squeezed her shoulder as she drove. To make her laugh, I confessed quite truthfully that I liked country music. To be equally open, Ophelia admitted to me that she liked "twang, twang" music too. We swore each other to secrecy, then drove the rest of the way to World's End State Park, happily singing golden oldies from all the "somebody done somebody wrong" radio stations, which we now defined as the blues–country style.

When we got back, I was ready to introduce Ophelia to Wydia. Wydia wasn't exactly thrilled at the prospect.

"She thinks she's what?" Wydia exclaimed when I first broached the subject. Wydia was gathering Senegalese earrings and Kenyan prints to take to the Afro-American bazaar at 23rd and South Streets. "You say this White girl you're seeing thinks she's what, Karen?" Wydia stopped folding Kente cloth long enough to slap her hands on her hips and swing her head around to eyeball me.

"Well," I said, backing off a few feet to give Wydia more space. "Ophelia doesn't really think she's Black." I felt a bit guilty. Wydia had a literal mind and you had to be careful how you presented any White woman to her, let alone one who hadn't had a White lover since she left home at fifteen. Things like that brought out the psych major in Wydia.

"So what's the problem then?" Wydia grabbed a piece of white material and began wrapping her head, looking in the mirror over the table where she kept her goods displayed when she wasn't out on the circuit. "Is she just into denying her White skin privilege? Besides, girlfriend," Wydia said, swiftly turning from the mirror to face me, "I thought you were tired of White women and the women's movement."

"I'm tired of White racists—I don't have racist friends."

"I thought you needed a lover you didn't have to explain the Black experience to, someone you could call 'blood.' You said love relationships with White women required too much work."

"Well," I said, "that's true of most White women—but Ophelia's different."

"I don't know, Karen, I got too many things to do to be reserving time to spend with White women who think they're Black."

"You've got to meet her. You know what?" I raised my left hand, "I swear she reminds me of you."

"You want me to tell you quite honestly what I think of this, sugar?" Wydia asked.

I hesitated. Wydia had been my best friend since we met at an Afro-American Studies conference shortly after I got out of high school. Generally she couched harsh criticism in language that wasn't devastating, but frankly I didn't know if I wanted her to be honest this time. Wydia felt about White women the way I felt about White men. She didn't dislike them, they just didn't come up on her computer.

I decided to sidestep the question. "Where's your curiosity?"

"It's waiting downtown beside a vendor's license I was supposed to have picked up a half hour ago." She glanced at her wristwatch.

"Listen, I trust this woman," I said, calling in an old chit.

Back in 1973 when Wydia and I discovered and affirmed that Black was beautiful, we spent a few months exploring each other's bodies. Wydia was the first to figure out that our love for each other was best expressed in non-sexual terms. But before she got around to telling me, we both met Kudah. Kudah was a serious Black brother who had just come back as an exchange student to the Ivory Coast. When we first met him, he used to hang out with us, going to the theater and the Black history seminars. Once, at Freedom Theater, I discovered Wydia holding Kudah's hand in the darkened theater. When I complained about it during the intermission, she responded by covering their hands with Kudah's dashiki. It hurt. I cried; we argued. But because our love for each other was greater than lust, our friendship remained whole and strong.

"Wydia, this is not your typical honky." I used the word honky even though it no longer expressed the way I felt about White women, so Wydia could see we were still on the same side as when I'd admired Kudah for his arrogance, for his insistence on defining who he was as good, and fighting for the definition. "She's White but she has excellent Black consciousness," I said.

"You asked me to trust you, then you tell me this White woman who's had forty years of White skin privilege has excellent Black consciousness?"

"Yes," I said doggedly. "Ophelia ran away from home at fifteen and she's been raised by the parents of her Black friends ever since. When Ophelia introduces you to her 'family,' she takes you to 17th and Bainbridge and presents you to Pookie Brown's family. She calls them her former in-laws."

"This Pookie, was she a stud?"

"Stud???"

"Well, you know. . . . " Wydia looked embarrassed, "someone who identifies with men."

"Well maybe, but Ophelia's nobody's femme. I couldn't be bothered with someone like that. They expect you to be John Wayne." I didn't know why I was getting angry. "And what the hell does that have to do with anything anyway?"

"I just don't want you to be jerked around by some silly-ass White girl who doesn't know what she's about."

"Okay, so now I'm a victim? Now I need you to protect me?" I shoved my hands into my pockets. "I'm going to tell you something, Wydia." I could be real frank when I was angry. "I never liked Kudah. Now, I'm not talking about the jealousy part, I got over that. But I've always felt Kudah was arrogant and sexist. And he spent too much time trying to get you to buy into polygamy. But I've always been polite to him because you like the guy and I respect you enough to support you in decisions you make for yourself. If that doesn't work both ways, I've misunderstood our relationship."

"Take it easy," Wydia said. She walked over and placed her hand on my shoulder, gave me a half smile and straightened the kumfe on my head.

I was sorry I'd let her have it that way.

"Why don't you fix me some of those stir-fried veggies and rice and I'll be over Wednesday to meet your girlfriend. Seven o'clock okay? Maybe I'll bring Kudah."

. . .

Wydia arrived at my house for dinner only fifteen minutes late. This was a major concession for Wydia who seemed to feel that punctuality was something designed by "the man" to keep Blacks in their place. Kudah came too, as sharp as you please in complete traditional attire, even down to the kumfe which he declined to remove for dinner. I wore my traditional jeans but they were designer and brand new, a recent gift from Ophelia. I also wore my "Dykes on Bikes" T-shirt which Kudah hated. Ophelia traded her usual flamboyance for a light blue blouse with puffy sleeves, designer jeans and flat shoes.

We converged around my dining room table to eat off my best china on a white linen tablecloth imported from Ophelia's house.

Wydia didn't waste time, choosing her words carefully. "So how does a White woman get to be an officer in a Black women's social group?" Wydia asked for the butter then stopped, stared at Ophelia. The bread and butter knife was still poised in her hand.

"Man, you are one tough cookie," Ophelia said with a giggle. She poured herself some wine, sat with her elbows on the table and returned Wydia's steady stare. "Okay," Ophelia said, getting serious now. "It's because I care about working against racism more than they do."

"That's true," I chimed in, "Zodiac is definitely a party hearty group. They'll be talking about institutional racism and somebody'll mention some joint, the next thing you know Zodiac women'll be scrambling from the table yelling, 'Where? Where?'" I couldn't resist taking a shot at Blanche and the women from Zodiac. They treated me like an interloper who had an unearned "in" with Ophelia.

"Yeah, but I bet you wouldn't catch any of them dead at some White girl's poetry reading," Ophelia shot back.

"Touché," I said, holding up my beer filled wine glass.

Having taken care of me, Ophelia returned her attention to Wydia, with occasional glances over at Kudah. "See, I view Zodiac as an avenue by which I can fight racism," she said. "Quite frankly I was hoping this was something Karen and I could work on together. Besides," she said with a giggle, "the only Black group they'd let me join is one I start from scratch."

"Moses here gonna lead the Israelites out of Egypt," I said flippantly.

Ophelia gave me a long hurt look. I ate another bite of broccoli and chicken and decided to keep my mouth shut for awhile. Ophelia poured some wine into Wydia's empty glass. Wydia too was getting giggly.

I was surprised to find Ophelia flirting. From time to time she'd touch Wydia's hand and give her that "you're the only special person in the world" look. I was touched by Ophelia's instantaneous and sincere affection for my best friend.

"The truth is that I really don't like White people," Ophelia said, putting down her wine glass. "If I'm going to be actively anti-racist it's got to be with the sisters, 'cause White girls get on my nerves. I'm going to tell you something funny," she said, grinning even before she began. "I once went to this one day workshop in which this White woman wrote this song. She'd apparently had what she felt was the pleasure of fucking this musician, a brother of course. And the White girl managed to offend everyone—White women, Black women—even Black men—the bitch offended everyone by singing this song entitled—and I swear I did not make this up... ," she fell on the table laughing, "Black Dick Frenzy." She let out a loud burst of laughter. Some of the giggling, I suspect, was due to the wine. "Now I ask you, are White girls fucked up or what?"

Ophelia continued without waiting for a response. "Later in the evening this chick and I got to talking and I suggested as delicately as possible, that maybe she should not have sung the song in front of a mixed audience—see, I can be nice to White girls too, like my liberal friend here," she said, pointing to me. Ophelia threw me a kiss and I looked to see what kind of reaction the "Black Dick Frenzy" story was having on Kudah and Wydia. I couldn't tell.

"The song offended everybody," Ophelia continued, "and the woman seemed genuinely bewildered as to why everybody was so upset. I guess her mind was still clouded by the frenzy." She broke up laughing again.

"You sit there and put down White women," Kudah said, "but have you looked in the mirror lately?"

"Yeah, but that's all external, outer trappings. The inner me is Black. You know," she said almost shyly, "you can think of me as a reverse Oreo; White on the outside, Black on the inside." She giggled again and reached down by her chair for her shoulder bag. "You guys mind if I smoke?"

Nobody said yes; but nobody said no, either. So Ophelia rolled a thick joint and handed it to Kudah, who took a drag and handed it to Wydia. Wydia waved it off and gave Kudah a look I couldn't decipher.

"I want to work with Black political activists," said Ophelia, exhaling a puff of smoke towards the ceiling. "But I don't want to have to spend most of my time proving I'm for real."

Wydia looked at me, at Kudah, then back again at Ophelia. Then she looked at me again. Questioningly. "Unless a Black person has a romantic personal interest in you," Wydia said, "I can't imagine anyone with strong ties to the Black community being willing to risk possible ostracism from the community to try to find a Black group in which you could be the only White person."

"And I couldn't do that anyway," I said. "All-Black space is important to many Blacks—at times I know it is for me—and I'm certainly unwilling to violate that space for another Black woman who feels a similar need."

"Of course I wouldn't violate anybody's space," Ophelia said. She wore the same hurt expression as when I'd made the crack about leading the Israelites out of Egypt.

During the shrill silence that followed, I remembered an incident which had occurred several weeks ago. Ophelia and I were sitting on a bench in the park not far from her house when two White teenaged boys drove by in a beat-up Chevy and called Ophelia a "cunt-lapping nigger lover." Ophelia had picked up a fallen tree branch, reached for my hand, and said in her usual non-threatening way, "That's right, motherfucker, I love this nigger." I would have loved to report that incident now but I knew it would not have gone over. There were some verbal boundaries beyond which White folks could not cross. The word "nigger" was one of those boundaries. I brought up the subject of sports. Kudah and I ragged on Mike Schmidt and Larry Bowa a bit and the tension passed. For fifteen minutes everything was alright. We talked about Alex Haley's *Roots,* and Ophelia regaled us with another humorous story about Pookie. Then, in passing, Ophelia said she went by "C.P." time. The words stuck out like a roach on the white linen tablecloth. Wydia registered disapproval first. She laid her fork on her napkin and sat up straight. "What do you mean by 'C.P.' time?"

Usually Ophelia reserved homegrown Black expressions for those Blacks who knew and accepted her inner self. This was a wrong move in a carefully orchestrated chess game with Kudah and Wydia.

"Well, I see myself as Black and therefore I can say I go by Colored People's time," Ophelia said with that disarming smile. Leave it to Ophelia to take the offensive.

"The hell you can," Kudah said, standing up now.

"The hell I can't," retorted Ophelia. She too was standing up but, unlike Kudah, she was still smiling. I marveled at her ability to fend off hostility with a smile. "I earned that right," she said, nodding her head firmly, "I'm paying my dues right now." She had both hands on her hips. I stood up too, just in case things got physical. Finally Wydia got up and suggested that everybody sit down.

A telephone operator with a heavy Southern drawl woke me with a collect call from a pay telephone in North Carolina.

"Since you're at least part of the reason I couldn't sleep, I figured it was okay to wake you up." I heard Ophelia's soft giggle through the receiver and felt myself smiling. I imagined her standing in a phone booth in front of a general store smiling her enigmatic smile, a lightweight jacket on her shoulders to protect her from the September chill. I sat up on the side of the bed so I could wake up completely.

"I guess that means you're not still mad at me, huh?"

I recalled our last argument, the one we had after Wydia and Kudah stormed out of my apartment a month ago. What was it about anyway? The Phillies, middle-class mentality? I couldn't recall and it didn't matter anyway. I was tired of coddling her, of being on the defensive. The relationship had become hard work.

"You *are* a damn White girl!" I had screamed at her. I'd never forget the expression on her face—as if I had suddenly back-handed her without provocation.

"It always comes to this doesn't it?" she'd asked.

What could I have said? I didn't want to hurt her, but this was crazy. "You're not Black, Ophelia. You're sweet and warm and you're real important to me, but you are not Black."

"It's not like I don't know that," she said so softly I could barely hear her. "And it's not like you don't know I know that. Pookie and I fought like cats and dogs," Ophelia had continued in that same distant voice, "but she never once called me a White girl, not after she got to know me. Not once after that."

"Ophelia, I can't be anybody but myself," I'd said. She was sitting on the couch; I was on an ottoman a few feet away. There didn't appear to be a way we could reach each other across the vast distance. Then Ophelia had come up beside me. She'd held me and I'd held her and we both cried. Now, as I sat on the side of my bed staring at my bare feet, I waited for Ophelia to say if she was still mad at me.

"No, I'm not mad at you, Karen." She spoke in a voice that suggested something more devastating, more permanent had taken place. "I want you to know," she added, "that I wasn't sleeping with anyone else when we were lovers. You do believe that, don't you?"

"Yeah, sure," I said. "That's one of the things I love most about you, your honesty." I noted the past tense in her reference to our relationship but decided not to comment. With a barely discernible prick of jealousy, I thought of Pookie Brown and remembered the lyrics of an old song about a love affair being too hot not to cool down. I opened my mouth to say 'I love you; be happy' but the words came out, "Have you been in touch with Pookie Brown?"

"That's all part of my past now, Karen. I've been trying to find out where I belong, or if there's any place where I truly belong. All I've found out so far is that you can never go home again. The people I stayed with when I first ran away from home are in New Jersey now. I'm going to look them up, go out to Chicago to visit my sister and then I guess I'll decide what I'll do from there."

"You'll give me a call when you come back this way?"

"Of course. I'll never forget you, Karen."

Epilogue

I saw Ophelia again yesterday, the first time in two years. She was behind a makeshift vendor's stand at an Afro-American festival on Belmont Plateau in Fairmount Park. She was surrounded by large pots and was selling fried chicken sandwiches and some kind of lentil and peanut soup from the Ivory Coast. I blinked and shook my head. This was not the Ophelia I had known and loved. Not the wild, flamboyant Ophelia who wore red spiked heels and mini skirts to women's conferences. I could not believe that the arrogant woman who crossed streets against the red light was standing there dressed in the traditional submissive black attire of Moslem women. I walked several steps across the grass towards Girard Avenue. Then I heard what could only have been Ophelia's infectious laugh. I turned, walked back, stepping aside to make way for an older woman pushing a baby in a pink stroller. I threaded my way through the throngs of dashiki-clad Afro-American men and women. Involuntarily I found my way back to the stand as one's tongue invariably finds its way back into the cavity of an abscessed tooth. I had to speak to her.

"Ophelia!" I called.

She smiled, held up a finger signaling 'one moment.' I watched as she handed a large woman in cornrows a veggie burger, then she turned to me.

"Naimah," she corrected me. "I'm Naimah now. But how've you been, Karen?"

"I'm sorry," I said awkwardly.

"No problem. I want you to meet my sister-wife. Here, Jasmine, meet my friend Karen."

"Pleased to meet you, Jasmine," I said, forcing a weak smile. Jasmine wore the same black outfit from head to toe as did Ophelia. A carmel colored woman in horn-rimmed glasses, Jasmine smiled at me then went back to waiting on a skinny adolescent who was waving a ten dollar bill over his head.

Ophelia passed Jasmine a brown paper bag. "That'll be two dollars," she said as Jasmine passed a sandwich to a pair of ebony hands. "You just missed Kudah," she said, turning back to me. "He just left to pick up some pita bread."

I had known they were lovers, that they'd gotten together after Wydia and Kudah broke up, but I couldn't believe Ophelia's transformation.

"You guys gonna make Wydia's wedding in September?" I asked.

"I don't know," she said shyly. "Kudah and Jasmine will probably go but. . . " She shrugged her shoulders and clutched desperately to a silly smile on her face.

I was embarrassed for her. "So, how've you been?" I asked.

"Oh, just fine." She brightened visibly. "I'm pregnant.

Three months," she said, rubbing her round stomach. The smile spread to include her eyes. "I've always wanted a child of my own."

I bought a fried chicken sandwich and found myself saying, "I guess Nijah and I will have to have you over for dinner one night." I wasn't sure why I said that except that it seemed like a nice thing to say. Or maybe because I wanted a gentle way to tell Ophelia I was into a good relationship with a strong Black woman.

"That would be nice, Karen," Ophelia said. "I guess you're pretty happy now too, huh?"

"Yes, Ophelia," I said, "I am happy." And I leaned over the stand and hugged that White woman right there under the disapproving gaze of all my Afro-American brothers and sisters, waiting in line for food.

Voyages Out 2

Nona Caspers

"Está bien"

I met Jesus once, in Guatemala. He was traveling light—a robe, sandals, and a backpack. It was in a little village on Lago de Atitlan. A village without roads. I was hiking around the lake, and there he was, helping the villagers make rope out of a type of plant I forget the name of. All day they pounded and twisted and wove the fibers together to make the strongest, smoothest rope I'd ever seen. I knew the man was Jesus right away because of the pictures I'd seen, and he had that same passive look on his face. There were, of course, holes in his feet and palms.

I asked him, What is your name? *"Cómo se llama?"* And he made no ceremony over answering, I am Jesus. Of course he said this in Spanish, *"Yo soy Jesús."* I nodded my dusty gringa traveler's head and sat on my own backpack to watch them weave rope into the night. Then I asked about a place to string up my hammock, and Jesus invited me to share the hut they had made for him.

I played my recorder while he meditated. Then we talked about the weather and about my travels and his much longer ones, and then I asked him some questions, since I figured this may be the only time in my life to get uncensored answers. First I asked him about some contradictions in the Bible, which he'd never read. I'm not much for reading, he said, of course in Spanish, *"No leo mucho."*

And I nodded, though I am much for reading, and at the time was reading the sixth book in the *Chronicles of Narnia*. I asked him if he wanted me to read a chapter to him, but he said, No thanks. *"No, gracias. Tengo que dormir. Mucho trabajo mañana."* Much work tomorrow. And, of course, I understood, but before we went to sleep, I did take the opportunity to mention that I was lesbian, just to see his reaction. I was at the stage of coming out to everyone. I don't know what I expected, but Jesus only nodded with his eyes half shut and said, That's nice. *"Está bien."* And went to sleep.

Now I was only 19 at the time, with my intestines full of bugs and my ears full of dust, so I could have misunderstood the whole situation; but I swear he said, *"Está bien."*

The next morning Jesus got up before the sky to make rope while me and my bugs slept in. When I woke and packed my bag, the whole village was out of sight, working in a different part of the forest. I trudged on to the next village where the people fed me boiled green weeds. *"Coma. Coma."*

I have always remembered the words of Jesus. Especially the last ones.

When I First Kissed Marsha from the Brady Bunch on the Lips and the Truth about Why the Series Ended

It all began in 1976 when my older sister went off to college and had a lesbian experience with a woman named Arianna who came to the Midwest from Rhode Island. I was in the sixth grade. My sister brought Arianna home with her one weekend to witness her authentic working class rural upbringing. I brought my friends over to watch *The Brady Bunch* on TV and eat Trix cereal dry out of the box. Mom and Dad were at the turkey factory. My sister stood behind us in the kitchen with her arms folded and she nodded to Arianna as if to say, "see the squalid place from which I sprout." Then she told me and my friends that if the sugar didn't destroy our minds and molars sitting so close to the TV would make us blind and subject to further discrimination in this rich white sightist male world. I shrugged and inched closer to the screen. The Tang commercial ended, the theme song began, Marsha Brady appeared in the Brady's large front living room and my sister strode forward and hit the power knob shouting, "Turn that crap off!"

But Arianna from Rhode Island winked and mumbled, "Aw, let them watch. Marsha Brady's one of us."

I turned to look at my sister's strange friend who just then kissed my sister on the lips. Us? Us? Then I turned back to my program. Upon my sister's arrival she'd taken me aside and announced that her and Arianna would be sleeping in my bedroom in the same bed because they were having a lesbian experience and that lesbians were women who loved women, not men. Now I wondered... was this the real reason for Marsha Brady's vague phony interest in the boys she was supposedly dating and not, as I once feared, that Marsha Brady was a vague phony character?

I started telling all my friends that the oldest daughter of Mr. and Mrs. Brady was a lesbian. We watched her closely for signs. What did lesbians in California do? What did lesbians in California eat? What did lesbians in California say? What TV programs did they watch?

My friend Karen questioned my authority, "Are *you* sure?"

"Yes, Karen," I huffed. "What would you know about it anyway, has anyone in your family ever had a lesbian experience?"

"Well. No." She had to admit.

The next day I begged my mother and father (who worked all day gutting giant hormone-fed turkeys then came home and fell asleep over soggy turkey TV dinners) for cable TV. "Ya, sure," they said, confident that with my sister's college education she would someday make enough to support us all. Now I watched the Brady Bunch morning, noon and night. In the morning I watched over Froot Loops, after school I watched over Trix and in the evening I watched over the snores of Mom and Dad. In my own sleep I began singing *The Brady Bunch* theme song... *then they fell in love and made a family....* Every night I had the same dream. The August Angel which sat on the head of my bed to protect me was really Marsha Brady. She would fly around the room like Tinker Bell and then I would wake and she would sprinkle me with fairy dust and we would whiz to California and Alice would set another plate on the large dining room table for me and we'd eat roast beef and fresh buttered carrots and baked potatoes and everyone would say please and thank you and no one would fall asleep and after supper Marsha would take me outside and tell me all her problems and I would solve them all and be granted a kiss on the lips.

I began dressing like Marsha Brady, wearing my hair like Marsha Brady, taking trivial things seriously like Marsha Brady and following my mother around the house asking such things as, "Gosh, Mom, do you think I should apologize to Fred at school for taking his pencil?"

I soon realized that I was in love. I made a list:

WHAT MARSHA BRADY AND I HAVE IN COMMON
   1.) Dull wardrobe.
   2.) Dull life.

Then I made another list:

WHAT MARSHA BRADY AND I DON'T HAVE IN COMMON
   1.) Her family has a maid.
   2.) She's a fictional character/I'm a real human being.

There were moments when I thought it would never work. I would never taste those palm tree lips, never be accepted as a legitimate member of the Brady household, never see California; I was doomed to a loveless Midwestern reality and permanently exhausted parents. Once, after they were well into sleep over *Turkey with Brownie,* I threw my lips against the blue glow of the TV screen just as Marsha looked up from her homework. All I tasted was dust and glass.

It was certainly time for some action.

On a lonely afternoon about three months later I finally trapped fate in my palms, stole my father's turkey factory paycheck and bought a one-way ticket west. At the California airport I looked under B in the telephone book and there it was in bold letters: MARSHA BRADY OF THE BRADY BUNCH. I dialed the number and the voice of my dreams answered, "Hello, Brady residence."

"Marsha, Marsha is it really you? This is Nona from the Midwest. I'm in love with you!"

"Oh, hi, Nona. Would you like to come over for dinner at my house? Alice is making a really good stew."

I accepted the invitation, abandoned my parka, donned a sun dress and a dab of patchouli oil which my sister had sent me in the mail. The taxi dropped me off at the end of the driveway. The Brady house looked just like the house on the television program—large and expensive. Bobby answered the door all smiles. "Oh, hi." Then he screamed, "Marsha!" In another moment there she stood in front of me. Golden hair, blue eyes, her hands behind her back and grinning in that shy little way of hers.

"Won't you come in."

I stepped inside the spacious living room and followed Marsha to the kitchen where she introduced me to her family.

"Mom. Dad. This is Nona from the Midwest and she came all the way from Minnesota to stay with us forever."

"My goodness aren't you a brave little girl," Mr. Brady said as he snuck a carrot from the tray Mrs. Brady was arranging with the fresh vegetables Alice was cutting.

Mrs. Brady smiled at me. "Alice, do you think we have enough food for a hungry traveler?"

"Oh, I'm sure we can fill her stomach to her chin, Mrs. Brady," Alice joked.

"Well, I'm not that hungry," I told them. Marsha laughed and I could feel her feathery split ends brush my bare shoulder. "Alice lives to serve our family and our family's friends," she said. Then in ran Cindy hollering about Jan taking her seat in the family TV room but Mrs. Brady calmed them down.

"What are you watching?" I asked.

"*Eight is Enough.*" Cindy answered with a slight lisp. Marsha led me to the family room, and there the rest of the Bradys sat watching the Bradfords on TV. After the program was over Mrs. Brady called us into the dining room for supper. Alice set a plate for me between Marsha and Peter who sat next to Greg; Jan, Cindy and Bobby were on the other side. There was beef stew, baked potatoes, fruit salad, avocados and broccoli and if anything was missing we could just ask Alice. Everybody chewed with their mouths closed and said things like "Please pass the butter, sister." "No problem, brother." The meal was going along quite smoothly when suddenly Peter put his fork down and said:

"Mom. Dad. I have something I need to say to the family."

"OK, Peter. We're all listening, what is it?" It was Mr. Brady's voice at the head of the table to my left. We all turned to Peter who was shifting around on his chair.

"Well, I just want to tell you all something very important about myself that I've never told anyone ever before."

"Yes Peter, go on." I could see Mr. Brady catch Mrs. Brady's eyes at the other end of the table.

"Here goes... " Peter reached one hand to his head and peeled off his thick curly black hair to show a pink head of skin and a multi-colored fluorescent tattoo on one side that resembled the letters KKK.

"Oh, Peter, when did you do that?" Mrs. Brady pursed her lips.

"Last week. I wanted to tell you but I thought you'd be mad."

"We're not mad, Peter," Mr. Brady assured. "We're

just glad you thought you could trust us enough to be honest. It never pays to lie. Now put your hair back on before Alice sees you."

Peter pulled his hair back on. I swallowed the hunk of fat from the roast that had momentarily caught in my throat.

"Does anyone else have anything to say?" Mr. Brady asked, scanning the faces of his children around the table.

"I do, I do." It was Bobby, wiggling in his seat and waving his hands. "Mom. Dad. I've joined the Divine Light Mission and won't be coming home after school."

Mr. and Mrs. Brady sighed. "Is it what you really want, Bobby?"

"Yes."

"OK, son. But remember, when you do something, you should always try to do your best."

"Thanks Mom. Thanks Dad. God is all, God is bright, God is electric in my soul."

Now I noticed Cindy squirming in her seat.

"Cindy. . . . " Mrs. Brady said sternly. "What's wrong?"

"It's just. . . this." And out from under the table she pulled 4 pairs of designer jeans, a child-sized mink coat and a diamond watchband.

"Oh, Cindy!" Mrs. Brady shook her head. "You've been stealing again. What did we tell you last time?"

Cindy hung her golden curls into the gravy. "No TV for a month," she lisped. I rubbed my eyes and wondered if my sister was right about Trix and television—obviously my mind was deteriorating along with my vision.

"That's right, young lady, and you know you'll have to bring it all back."

"I will," Cindy whined. "Promise." Her curls soaked

up the beef gravy dissolving her platinum blonde dye which oozed into her clump of potatoes. I pushed my well-balanced meal away and stared around me in horror. Criminals, Neo-Nazis and cult junkies smiled back at me. Was this The All American Family?

"Greg, Jan, Marsha, have you got anything to tell us?"

I waited, horrified that I'd find out my Marsha was a Communist spy, a heroine junkie and a baby snatcher! Marsha smiled serenely, taking my limp hand under the table. "No Mom. No Dad. Everything's fine."

"Oh sure, you little miss goody two shoes!" Jan threw her dirty napkin across the table into Marsha's face.

"I am not a goody two shoes, Jan, I just don't have any pressing problems this week."

"Oh you never do and do you know why?" Jan sneered, "Because you're a vague, phony, inane character."

"That's just not true, Jan." Marsha tried to reason. Jan gave her the finger. Marsha stuck out her tongue. Jan grabbed it and started twisting.

"Break it up girls, break it up." Mr. Brady rose from his place and placed a firm but gentle hand on each girl's shoulder. "Jan what's this all about?"

"Well since you two won't help me pay back the loan I had to take out for my cocaine addiction and since crack deals are going slow I've had to take up dominatrixing on the side." Jan crumpled into tears. I gasped. Mrs. Brady smiled empathetically and joined Mr. Brady behind Jan.

"Oh Jan, is that all?" Mrs. Brady said and gave her a hug.

Mr. Brady returned to his seat. "It's OK, Jan. We understand. Just don't let it interfere with your homework." He surveyed the table again. "Now children is there anything else?"

We all shook our heads. Mine felt like it would fall off

on my plate. Marsha squeezed my hand under the table. Her skin was as smooth and cool as my old Casey doll who came with six different wigs. Peter's wig was slightly askew.

"Excuse me," I said shyly. "Is there a bathroom in this house?"

After supper the family went back into the TV room to watch another episode of the Bradfords while Alice cleaned up the mess singing and tap dancing from kitchen to table. I was trying to signal Marsha to go outside so we could be alone. I needed to talk. But she was engrossed in the program which was one of the first in the series.

"What a nice family," she said.

"God is divine, God is light, God is electric," chanted Bobby.

"Fuck you," Jan yelled and sniffed.

I nudged Marsha's shoulder and whispered, "Do you think we could go outside for a moment?"

"Oh. Sure. Mom. Dad. Brothers and sisters. Nona and I are going to go outside for a moment." She announced. They waved us on. "Have a good time."

In the Brady backyard there was evenly mowed grass and a picnic table.

"Just look at that moon," Marsha mused with her hands behind her back. "Do you think there's really a man on the moon?"

I looked up and saw an anorexic moon pasted in a manic glittering sky. "I heard my sister and Arianna say it was a woman," I answered.

"Hmmm," Marsha said.

"Wow, Marsha, your family's pretty messed up, isn't it? Thank goodness you're normal... aren't you?"

"Oh, yes, I've always been normal. My character was made that way."

She smiled at me then, and led me to stand under the tangerine tree near the fence in the corner. Her breath smelled like tangerines.

"Um. Marsha. Before we go any further. Do you think you'd want to come stay with me and my family in the Midwest?"

Marsha Brady put one hand on my shoulder and soon I felt the heat of her palm tree lips over mine.

CHICKEN-DYKE

We had not come innocent to this dim bar with the Brigadoon mist of Marlboro smoke under strobe lights. Our eyes were still adjusting, but our goal was clearly set. I mean, my goal. Tonight I would ask some strange woman to dance. Just one dance, nothing more. A fast one where we didn't even have to smell or look at each other but could just flail around in similar space. Jane, my best friend, was here to offer her immoral support. Jane had firm principles and a big lap. She also hated to dance, so if I wanted to, which I always did, I'd have to ask someone else.

I was not shy in a general way, nor was I new to lesbian culture; I had been practising for years. The problem was, or so I had recently discovered in therapy, that I had developed a survival pattern that was beginning to interfere with my personal growth: fuck first, dance later; fed by a deep fear of reflection. After 48 hours in bed who can think about consequences and compatibility. And, of course, by that time, I was fairly sure they'd say yes. Both Jane and my therapist agreed that I should try something different this time. My last six relationships had ended in lesbian disaster: we were surgically separated, then ripped each other's stitches out one by one. Still, the thought of asking a woman to dance without having touched the wet

warmth of her soul gave me the holy chills. It seemed easier to be naked and panting with a stranger, then fully
clothed and thinking.

The bar, "Sappho's Thigh," was semi-full with the
usual 80s assortment of dykes. Huddled over tables near
the speakers were the neatly muscled and outfitted prep
dykes, with strong jaws and well-prepared tans. Up a step
from them, barely visible on their platform of smoke and
alcohol fumes, were the pool dykes, a bit messier, with
flabbier muscles, jaws, and tans that wouldn't make it to
December. In the middle of the room, avoiding the speakers and the bar, sat the sober feminist dykes, wearing natural fibers, drinking Cold Spring and waving pale hands at
lung cancer. Dispersed among these groups were random
clumps of violent femme funk dykes, with ragged-edged
smiles, asymmetrical do's and fashionable bald spots. In
theory, Jane and I fit somewhere between the last two: we
were sober, and asymmetrical.

"I don't see anyone," I whispered in Jane's direction.
She leaned back and patted my arm.

"Keep looking."

I had made her promise not to let me slip into the quagmire of old behavior.

"There's at least fifty women in here," Jane com-
mented.

"And twenty-five couples," I mumbled back. I was not
up to challenging the monogamous status of anyone's relationship.

A new group of funk dykes strolled in with wild hats
and off-beat laughter. They scattered across the dance
floor and corramed like electrocuted bugs. Cute, I
thought, but too young. I had my limits. Scanning the
room again, I spied a familiar group of five women at a
table close by; four of them swooned in a purple haze,

leaving one woman obviously unloved. I looked closer. The slant of her hairline triggered a raw memory of my fourth lover. These associations lowered my pick considerably.

"Hey, what about her?" Jane suddenly poked me with her soft mocha fingers.

"Which her?"

"The short white woman that walks like an Irish Setter."

A woman in natural fibers and dangly earrings padded down the lavender aisle and sat at a table nearby, alone.

"She looks harmless," Jane said, and I watched as the woman tapped her foot, staring vaguely at the dance floor.

"Go ask her," Jane prompted.

I sucked in some hovering smoke for courage and answered, "I will." But when I looked at the woman again my bladder flipped and my nostrils began swelling shut. Some call it "Love At First Sight." I call it "Fear of Foolhood."

"I can't," I squeaked and Jane gripped my damp pizza dough palm.

"Yes you can!"

"She'll say no."

"Then you'll ask someone else."

I nearly fainted. Even my eyeballs were sweating.

"I'll be humiliated!"

Jane slid closer and stuck her big face into mine. "Look," she said calmly. "There are a million reasons why that one dyke might say no. She may have warts between her toes, she may be tired, she may be a virgin, she may not like to dance—"

"Or she may think I'm a silly ugly cow." In grade school Tanya Goalltheway had teased me for walking like a cow.

"Forget about that Tanya what's her name. You don't believe, for one moment, that you are a silly ugly cow, do you?"

"I'm not sure."

"Well, now, listen to me. Put your skinny pink ear close to my mouth, I don't want to repeat this."

I followed her instructions and felt hot spittle tickle my ear drum.

"You are an attractive lesbian, dyke, and there are plenty of women who would love to dance with you—they go to bed with you don't they?"

"That's different. Going to bed is... pure."

Jane snorted. I quickly removed my ear.

"God help that you should have to get to know someone before fingering their clit. You kill me, now go on."

I laughed a bit too, which loosened the crust of fear gathering in my joints, and began bravely sliding my chair away from our table when, suddenly, the woman stood and walked toward the door.

"Too late. She's leaving." I settled back in, closer this time.

"She's going to the bar."

"Jane, I can't go out with someone who drinks," I hissed feverishly.

"Only dehydrated dykes can dance with you, huh? Girl, she may be ordering a Diet 7-up for all you know."

We held our breath as the woman's lips moved and the bartender handed her a bottle of mineral water. Jane slapped my back.

"Hah! She's cute, she drinks Perrier—what more do you want for one dance?" She nudged my chair.

"Don't push me, I'll go when I'm ready."

"You'll never be ready."

"It's my process!" I snapped, and Jane's head dipped

back, leaving the rest of her large body firmly planted.

"Honey, if somebody don't push you, you'll be sit'n on my lap root'n for milk soon." Her eyes noted my increasing proximity. I backed off a few inches.

"Well. . . how do we know she's not waiting for a date or something?"

"We don't. But she does." Jane nodded to the woman who was casually glancing around the room.

"I'm not sure I can take a no. I'm at a fragile point here. Jane?"

Jane's chin rested on her hands over the table as the strobe lights flashed in the whites of her eyes making them look like crystal balls. I knew she was thinking hard, because her neck folded up like a Supreme Court judge.

"Let me ask you some hypothetical questions," she began. "Suppose this woman, who I am beginning to pity, suppose she says no. One: Are you going to die?"

"No." I answered maturely as Michael Jackson tried to convince us of his low nature.

"Are you going to be depressed forever?"

"No."

"Are all your cotton clothes going to tumble down round your bony ankles and is your skin going to turn mustard yellow?"

"No, but—"

"Pea green?"

I laughed. "No. But I'll feel like a fool."

"Uh-huh. And for how long will you feel like a fool?"

"I don't know."

"But not forever, do you agree?"

"Yes. I mean, no, not forever."

"All right. So. The worst thing that could happen is that you'll feel a little foolish for a little while. And then, of course, this poor unsuspecting woman may say yes, god help her, and you'll get to dance instead of huddling next to my slumbering body and listening to me nag you up and down all night for being such a coward."

I took a long strong sip of my Diet 7-up, through the straw, and practiced reflecting. I could feel the Nutrasweet and Jane's words turning to formaldehyde in my stomach; churning and eating at my soul. The woman still sat at her table, tapping and taking dainty swigs on her Perrier.

"Op, look'it Jane, she's a femme," I motioned. "I won't be butch enough for her."

"God, girl, you are really reaching into history for rejection."

"I can't help it. It's such a big responsibility." I slumped onto the table, bumping my glass with my nose. Jane was heavily quiet. "I mean what if she's a closet case or what if she smokes or doesn't put the lids back on the honey jar or throw her envelopes away or—"

"Stop your whining! You are the chickenest woman I know." Jane smashed her lips together and skinnied her wide brown eyes. "Shit, you sound like you're asking her to marry you when all you're gonna do is dance." Then she said through her teeth. "That is all you're gonna do, right?"

"Yeah, but, who knows what will come of it." In my head I was already married, with two turkey-baster kids and a joint checking account, picking my way to the toilet through four inches of honey jar lids and envelopes. Then came the horrible break-up, the grief, the anxiety, skin withdrawal, phone calls in the middle of the night, the humiliating grovel for one last conflict.

"Ohhh." I moaned and buried my head in Jane's shadowy cleavage. She pinched me.

"You in there? Quick, pick it up. She's looking this way."

I peeked out from her virgin wool breast.

"Oh my god, get me out of here. Jane, she's looking at me," I hissed. "What am I going to do?"

"Try breathing and extracting your nails from my leg."

"Sorry." I sat up. "Oh, Jane, she smiled, wasn't that a smile?"

"Either that or she's got gas."

"OK. This is it. I'm going to do it." I announced. "It's just one dance, right? Nothing's going to change unless I do, right? I'm an adult, I've got a charge card. Oh, it's so exciting, I'm really going!"

"Hallelujah."

I rose from my chair like Joan of Arc and aimed my body toward hers. Then, suddenly, out of nowhere there appeared a second woman who walked like an Irish Setter and wore dangly earings. I slithered back on to my dead horse.

"That was close. See, she was waiting for a lover," I accused.

"Maybe." Jane leaned into one elbow like a yawn and studied the hypothetical couple. "They're not touching," she informed me.

"So it's a cold relationship."

Jane humphed and continued her study. I was ready to let my adrenaline glands sleep forever. I finished my 7-up in slow mindless sips, dreaming of a long orderly celibate life with narrow beds, empty metal wastebaskets and clean floors. Perhaps I'd join a silent cloister of nuns somewhere in the Himalayas.

"HAH!"

Jane's triumphant belch shattered my stale peace. I lifted my eyes to see that a third Irish Setter had attached her lips to the second, leaving number one clearly available. Well, it was no paltry kiss and my glands reawakened. Jane poked my arm.

"Now this IS it, girl, I'm sick of this shit! You don't want to ask her, fine. We'll just sit here all night and babble about important things like cloning in the lesbian community and... "

Jane's mouth froze as my knees began to clang under the table to the beat of a new attitude. I felt myself unfolding and as I rose from my chair I looked deep into my friend's warm eyes for some last boost of comfort.

"Jane? If it's no?"

"Then you crawl back into my arms and I'll carry you to safety."

"And if it's yes?"

I gulped her laughter like I used to gulp beer.

"Then you dance, say thank you, and steer your body back to this table. I'll be right here." She patted the synthetic mahogany table.

"OK. I'm off. This is it, Jane. Really."

My legs felt like water balloons, my stomach spilled acid like a faucet and I was sure that by the time I'd get there I'd be a halitosis wreck, I heard Jane whisper, "Go on, it's gonna be OK." and felt the wind from the back of her hand fanning me forward. Step by step I mucked across the hazy room, through the quagmire. When I finally reached her table I gripped the edge. My tongue lolled like a drugged fish against my teeth. The woman smiled up at me. I spoke.

"Dja... dja... uhhmm. Do you want to dance?"

"Sure."

As we moved onto the dance floor, I heard a distinct rumbling sigh from my table.

"You'll be getting my bill in the mail."

black bananas

October 13

    I was at M's house, visiting over mint tea in the bare white kitchen with that damn fluorescent light buzzing and glaring over our heads. M had a toothache. I was hungry. In the middle of the table there was a blue plastic plate stacked with Oreos. Last year at this time they would have been gone. Last year at this time B and I were in love. My palate is changing along with all the rest. Unrest?

While M was telling me about the gold bridge they were installing into her mouth and how the dentist marveled at the workings and shape of her lower bite, I had my eyes and thoughts on a bunch of bananas lounging on top of the fridge. I hadn't thought about bananas for years. These were firm, dark yellow—my favorite color, my next favorite color being B's pink skin, the next being my cat's black fur—and smooth, just ripe to eat. I suppose I could have asked for one, but they seemed private, ornamental, blessed.

later

Bananas are a stable fruit. Not like apples or oranges or

grapefruits or melons or grapes that roll off my spoon. Bananas are safe. You don't have to sniff at the bottom or squeeze them round the middle to test for quality like a cantaloupe. I've gotten bad melons, dull apples, sour oranges and pulpy bitter grapefruits, but I've never gotten a bad banana.

I remember eating bananas when I was little. There was a certain way to peel them—like on old Chiquita banana commercials—without breaking or crushing the tip or getting your hands sticky. I'd sit on the front steps, carefully peeling, then taking tiny bites and mashing the sweetness between my front teeth and tongue until it was like baby food. When I was done, my stomach would be full for hours and I'd lay on my back with the sun in my eyes and dream about some vague, safe, emotionless future with a husband, and kids, and dog, and family car.

even later

B lays next to me. In clothes. I am naked. Eyes dripping. Drip, drip, drip.

October 17

Rainy day. We met V and S for a late breakfast. We ate poached eggs, fried eggs, scrambled eggs and drank orange juice. I kept looking for whatever nutrient it is my body lacks these days, but it was not on the menu.

V told me I looked like a war victim. Maybe I am.

After breakfast V drove us to a flea market in the New Car. B and I sat in back, buckled close to our doors as if one of us might decide to jump out at any moment. I watched the gravel shoulder until it flowed like a river and my eyes hurt.

At the flea market I bought three bright green plastic bungy cords to attach to my window shades. I am tired of climbing onto chairs. It's part of my effort to make life easier, like trying to get a better job, moving the rug away from the doorway of the bathroom and taking Mega Vitamins—B Complex.

All the clothes at the market were piled on long narrow tables, cafeteria style. We dug and dug but everything seemed to be size three. As we were leaving, a tiny woman with orange lips chased me out the door yelling, "Thief! Thief!" and pointing a long fingernail at my heart. I showed her my receipt. She probably thought I was a drug addict or criminal with my black leather jacket and pink swollen eyes.

October 21

Went to work in a watery mood. Three years at the group home: housekeeping, wheelchair maintenance and transfers—renting out my extremities. Cheap.

There were some bananas on top of the residents' fridge. Why does everyone put them there? It's like some unspoken house rule. My mother always set them on top of a towel in the right front corner, as though they were on display. The bananas at work were bright yellow and still a little green at the stem. Every time I walked by I glanced at them. Somehow it seemed like if I just had a banana everything would be all right—B would stay, I'd find a better job, rugs wouldn't jam the doorways. . . .

Towards the end of the night, as I was sweeping the kitchen, I reached up, ripped one off and ate it while the residents were in the activity room watching *Dallas* reruns. (And I felt that long fingernail poking my conscience.)

Wild dream. I was caught shoplifting. One banana, but it turned into gold and they hauled me off screaming like a madwoman.

October 23

Out to eat again. Home seems small. Dishes. We went to a Chinese restaurant—B wasn't talking much so I memorized the Zodiac placemat. I am a "BOAR; noble and chivalrous." My friends will be life long, yet I am prone to "marital strife." Avoid other Boars, marry a Rabbit or Sheep. My opposite is the Cock.

October 27

Washed dishes finally. It is something that has to be done. I'm always surprised when they start overflowing their basin and take over the cutting board which means I can't open the fridge, unless I wash. I'm going to start doing them more often. Or maybe, if B leaves, I'll pack all the dishes away except one bowl, one spoon, one plate, one pot. . . .

October 29

B and I walked around the lake wrapped in pink and purple scarves. We talked until our noses dripped. We spread all our words on the frozen ground, then stepped on them, hearing syllables crack like thin sheets of ice. Our hearts breathed cold cold air. If I knew what to say to fix it, would I say it? Would green and kind words sprout out of my mouth?

After coming home from the movie with S and D and M (B went to a rug-making party) I sat on the sawed off sofa in my red pajamas and made lists. Lists of jobs to seek, classes to take, support groups to join, causes to support. Lists of cleaners and clothes and books and groceries to buy. If I write it all down, it makes me real. I will go on, all I have to do is look at a list, and one by one cross the items off. Then life moves on, like a cargo train loading and unloading.

My lists are my body guards, soul guards. They are my silver tracks. Monday you will do this, Tuesday that... and so on. On. On.

October 31

So now there are sun yellow bananas on top of my fridge—the right front corner, no towel. They look immediately comfortable and possessive, like the cat, only the bananas won't go into heat every month and trill from deep in the throat at the window or chew the corners of my papers.

later

The sun is out, the sky is crisp. I should go for a walk. Feed all that stale bread in the back of the fridge to those mixed-up ducks on the lake. They should be in Mexico by now. I wish they could talk, say something wise to me. Wise old ducks with bread-fat bellies. But they don't even quack much and when they do it doesn't sound like what's written in all those children's books. It sounds more like, "Waaaa. Waaaa."

November 3

I woke up to the sweet smell of bananas. I wrote with the

smell, dressed with the smell, shopped with the smell, watched the second half of *Another World* with the smell. Mary McLeary has come back from the dead with bright red hair and brown eyes. Vince called her a whore in the kitchen—there were bananas in a bowl on top of the fridge and he called her a whore. I shut it off. It's not as comforting now as when I was little and stayed home sick from school, sitting at my mother's feet while she ate grape jelly on pizza, watching the tears drain slowly out of Alice Mathew's blue eyes. My own eyes are dry. Things are getting better. Maybe B will stay. Do I want her to stay?

November 7

Writing is too hard. B. Gone.

November 8?

I got out of bed. My skin fell off. I spent the rest of the day with thimble and needle, trying to sew it back on.

November 9

B called. I wanted to fix our relationship like I'd fixed the toilet—by attaching a length of chain from my Saint Anthony medallion, B's heart to mine. It still wouldn't flush right. Afterwards I lay on my stomach over Mother's and Grandmother's quilts. Three layers of women with German thighs. Three tired women. Cat came and licked the crisis off my skin. I'd like to stay in bed until the year 2000, but I have to go to work, do the dishes, the laundry, vacuum, shop, make lists, scrub the toilet, call M about driving V to the airport, buy a new carburetor for the Valiant, pay my insurance. . . .

later

Whenever things got tough at work and I felt like my skin would slide off again, I thought about cat's pointy black face greeting me at the door of the apartment, and how I'd carefully peel one of those freckled bananas, then mash it slowly between my teeth and tongue until my stomach was full. I could almost taste it, but when I got home cat was asleep under the couch and I cut up an apple instead. It was a good apple, hard and sweet. B and I always ate apples with yogurt out of my big purple bowl before bed. Maybe that was our problem.

later later

(S called J called M called V called. They all say I will heal. All I want to know is when will I feel B's cheek on my shoulder, shoulder on my cheek, kiss to breast, breast, kiss.)

November 12

There must be something I can write about today that won't turn into B.

masking tape, crazy glue, rubber cement, rubber bands, magic wand.
bungy cord, patch kit, double stitch, twine, duct tape, magic wand.
Band-aid, Ben Gay, Banana, Tylenol, Benadryl, Magic Wand.

November 13

The freckles are now big fat brown blotches, growing together rapidly, like skin cancer. They're still edible. If nothing else I can use them for banana bread.

November 17

Frantic not to think of B's fingers folding paper, turning pages, picking the bacon off the pizza. The tears don't listen. They come when I'm going to the bathroom. They come when I'm trying to read. They come when I'm brushing my teeth, talking on the phone. They come when I'm at work trying to cut the chicken meat off the bone for the new resident so he won't choke to death.

Spent the day bending my thoughts to look like someone else's. Someone who can sleep at night. Someone who makes ten bucks an hour, twenty thousand a year. Someone who just bought a family car or dog or duplex. Someone whose insurance isn't due. Someone who can pay it. Someone who doesn't have five bananas rotting on top of their fridge.

I see them every morning and every night. Every time I open the fridge I think, you should eat a banana, but I don't.

November 20

The whole house stinks. The bananas are fermenting and evaporating through their blackening skin, curling, molding, hardening outside—inside brown liquid. I could squirt them into my mouth like they do in Mexico. Or I could throw the rotten things away. Damn. What a waste.

If B were here those bananas would have been eaten. Or out the door a week or two ago. If B were here. . . .

later

Maybe I can still make a liquado or something with them?

November 23

M came over. She showed me her gold bridge and I showed her my black bananas. "Why don't you throw them out," she asked, mouth gleaming under my 60 watt bare bulbs. (At least they don't buzz.) And I told her I was going to make something exotic with them. Her nose crinkled, "Throw them out, they stink."

We walked around the lake, fed the ducks and talked about life. We talked and talked and talked as though we had to figure things out today, under this cotton sky, passing this willow tree. We said the same things we said last year. The year before? Life is hard. Relationships are hard. Winter is cold. Too long. If only it ended in January. When will summer come (and it's not even December).

As we curved into the sun M said, "Nothing stays the same." I said, "They should have told us." She said, "They didn't know."

November 27

B came over to pick up some leftovers—left over tapes, socks, pictures, plants, silverware—untangling our possessions—didn't even notice the bananas.

We went to our favorite restaurant, sat in the same green booth and drank the same brown tea in white cups. I remembered the first night we walked around the lake and I lost my car keys so B had to spend the night. B remembered the different colors of my hair these last five years. We talked about my ideas for jobs and what she needs to do. I said some nasty things and B got quiet. Oh god, every hurt is piled up in my blood, I want this to end, I want everything better. I want someone to stay with me forever, 'til death.

When we said goodbye we hugged so tight I heard our ribs crack, like pistachios.

Now I lie on the hard floor and ask myself, were we really that rotten together? A small voice answers, "Yes."

Night

Oh god, this grief is so sharp I'm afraid I will cut myself on it.

Morning Finally Morning

I woke in a fist, hard against the wall. Loverless. I jumped up and dressed in steel, mouth like a trap set to spring. And those damn bananas! I don't even want to go into the kitchen.

Where are the kids, the dog, the family car, the driveway, the charge cards. Where is B!!

There's a lethal scream lodged in the center of my spine, in the back of my thighs, in the balls of my feet. I could go smashing through the roof of this apartment like a bullet.

I wrote "YOU WILL NOT DIE" in red marker on 15 recipe cards and taped them onto all my walls so that everywhere I look, I am reminded.

November 29

List of things I won't think about today:

B B B B Bananas Car Job

November 30 or 31

Too much energy in me for sitting and squeezing out words. I have to walk dance scream stretch roar.

December 3

I forced myself to go into the kitchen and look at them. Study their death. The ants have come in skinny rows. They march on invisible paths up the left shoulder of the fridge between the stacks of egg cartons (I don't know why I save those either) on to the flattened shriveled black juice. They march around the bunch, over it, through it and then carry some back to the colonies. The eaters and the workers. We should have it so tidy. Anyway, I am sort of glad that these ants have found the bananas. At least they are nourishing something in this house.

later

After work went dancing with M and J and S and V. I stomped imaginary ants with the toes of my orange boots and I kicked and I laughed. Came home to a mailbox full of bills, a letter from my mother and a red envelope from B. Inside was a single sheet of blue lined paper. It was a poem about me, us, the end. I read it over and over, sobbing. I read my mother's letter and sobbed some more, though all she did was tell me about the meal she and Dad ate at Embers last week.

I want to burrow to the bottom of the laundry basket, crawl inside the sleeve of my bright orange turtleneck and cry, or don't cry, but lay there and smell the body sweat, old skin and perfume.

December 7

No one B loves next will have a grey mole on the back of her neck. No one B loves next will have my breath, or my orange boots, or my stories.

December 11. Sunday night. Day off.

Strange day. This morning I brought the trash out. I set the bananas on top, then retrieved them, ants and all. I don't ask why. At the dumpster I ran into my neighbor who looked at me funny. "Hi, how are you doing?" "OK," I told him. I could have said, "I'm being eaten by obsessive thoughts, I hate my job, you've probably heard me screaming and sobbing through the walls and I can't seem to throw out a bunch of bananas that have been rotting for over a month. . . . " And he would have said, "Say, you know, they still haven't fixed my bathroom floor it's just a mess and they're thinking of raising the rent. . . . " I've heard it all before. Then, so has he. I forget that there is nothing new about breaking up. A million songs and poems and books written about it.

Before I left he did ask me what that smell coming from my apartment was. I told him I was making wine. His nose crinkled, like M's.

On my way back into the apartment I slipped on the ice and hit the back of my head on cement, throwing my brain against my forehead. My ears and eyes and cheeks began ringing, my nose dripped. I floated inside and sat at my desk with good intentions, but instead of going through the fine print of the want ads, I wrote and rewrote an eight page letter to B that made no sense at all, so I was told. I called V and J and M—read it to each one and they all said about the same thing: "You'd better call a doctor. Take a hot bath and lay down. Do you need anything?" M told me she thought my skull might have cracked and that the nose drips were brain fluid. She'd seen it on some medical show, or read it on the front page of the Enquirer— "Woman's Brain Leaks Out of Her Nose." It hurt to laugh. She also asked me if I'd thrown the bananas away yet. When I said no she said, "You know I love you." "Yes, I know."

I called the Doctor and the Doctor said, "Stay away from cigarette smoke, burnt toast, and small children with colds. Go to bed."

So now I'm in bed, wearing the red flannel pajamas M gave me for Xmas years ago, like arms wrapped around me. There is a path worn and rawness on either side of my nose above my lips. At the bottom of all these tears is a bucket of sky, a cat, and friends. M is coming to stay with me tonight.

December 13

Throw it off. Can't walk around dragging B like a tar shadow.

Dream

I am walking amidst a procession of friends who carry a sun yellow casket. B's name sticks out of it like one of those "Happy Birthday!" decorations stick out of a cake. The bearers are chanting something that sounds like, "Bla de bla, pray for us. . . "

December 17

Today I woke peaceful, the way cat wakes. The sky is sharp blue, I hear the ducks. All is as it should be. I should be alone in this apartment, with this cat, doing the dishes, going through the want ads. Those bananas should be black. I should be late to work. Nothing seems too tall or ugly. Not even thoughts of B with someone else could disturb me today. I feel far away from that. It was someone else, another time. We were other people.

I called all my friends and asked THEM how THEY were. Oh, and I have an interview on Friday!

Friday

interview went great. I am smart. I am smart. smart. smart. And beautiful. Who needs a family car.

January 3

Holidays over. Thank god. I made it through even without B's apple pies and presents. Am busy with new job. Come home exhausted, just want to rest and watch Nature programs.

M and I are taking a yoga class. Today I smiled like a nun or guru and said I was "blessed." M said, "You talk like anything good that happens is a deliberate grant from the Government or god." "It is," I said, "and I deserve it." She laughed as she twisted her leg behind her neck.

Yesterday I saw B waiting for a bus, wearing a shirt I'd never seen, never touched, and a hair style I didn't advise—who did? I won't think about that. The same blue eyes though. Darker than the sky. I crossed the street and said hello. I wanted to ask if I could have one or both of those eyes for a belated Xmas or New Years gift. "I've got a clean Wylers jar right here, just slip them in, thank you. Now I can look at them whenever I want."

Before I could actually say this, the bus came and carried B away.

Mrs. Hind's Yard

When I was in Junior High I mowed lawns to make some money to buy special items I knew I couldn't live without—like a motorcycle. Most of the people who hired me were old. Old women alone one way or another. If they had husbands living, they weren't living much. I would hear gutted moans or rattled breathing coming from the hallways of a few houses. And there were a couple of silent bodies propped up in tired chairs.

The women seemed to hang on. Most could get around, one way or another. They could always manage to get to the window to watch me mow. I remember them bent, lined faces almost pressed against the glass, squinting through cataracts and white glaze. Their eyes not at all afraid of mine. Some of the women used magnifying lenses or binoculars. It made me nervous. Stiff grey heads following me back and forth across the lawn, bobbing like one of those ceramo dogs with the hinged neck. When I was done they would knock knock knock, waving for me to come inside. It was like being forced to go on a class trip to a museum.

Once inside they'd press me into dust-filled, tired chairs in rooms where every bit of wall, every space, sagged full of memories which nobody wanted to hear. Especially a young girl in Junior High. I was too busy practicing the backflip and dreaming about the rides I'd give to all my girlfriends on the back of my motorcycle to listen to old women's stories about people I didn't know, half of them dead.

Mothers, daughters, fathers, sons, grandchildren, sisters... framed and placed, sometimes encased in glass cupboards next to filmy crystal and yellowing plastic memorial wreaths. Or hung on lime walls in rows—a regiment of posed smiling relatives who never visited, dead or not.

The women would serve me store bought cookies, the kinds I hated with raisins and white icing on top or vanilla wafers. Every mow they'd ask me the same questions: "How old are you now? What's your mother's maiden name? Why is such a pretty girl mowing lawns?" Then they'd give me a rundown on all those relatives row by row. Or I would get detailed accounts of bowel and bladder activity, leaks and creaks along with muscular aches and newly discovered patches of brown, purple and yellowed skin. These women warned me in serious voices: "Never grow old, never grow old." As if I could avoid it if I tried hard enough. If I was smart enough. Good enough.

At some point I would bring up the subject of money. Many seemed to have the notion that I mowed lawns for the state of my soul, or for the cookies. "Oh, you're such a nice girl, and so strong, to mow lawns for us old ladies. God bless you, have another cookie." When I reminded them of my charge—five to ten dollars a lawn—they'd look confused or flustered: "Oh yes. Let me see if I have any money." Then they'd pluck it out from under plants or disappear and come back with it. They handled the money like greasy car tools. Some of the pickier ones, with binoculars, would take this chance to point out spots that I missed and go on about how far the dollar went, and what did a young girl need with that much money? I didn't tell them about the motorcycle.

I sat through the disoriented looks, the disgruntled sighs and distasteful retrievals of the greenbacks. I knew I was worth it. Their lawns were the hardest to mow. Full of birdbaths, windflowers, plastic deer, holy statues in tubs and cumbersome little triangles filled with smooth speck-led rocks. I mowed around it all, without nicking.

One yard was particularly difficult. Mrs. Hind's. On her front lawn, year round, stood a manger scene. The grass loved to grow tall and thick around baby Jesus, who looked like a war victim—paint chipped, one eye pum-meled out by rain or picked out by squirrels and birds. Mary and Joseph were no longer stable in the stable. At the slightest bump of wind they would topple over like two drunks on a binge. They spent most of their time face down, killing the grass beneath them. All the shepherds were cracked.

Yet every two weeks I mowed carefully around their green stained feet. I picked up the unwed couple. I moved the holy baby's crib to clip the grass around it, the whole time feeling Mrs. Hind's sharp German eyes like nun's breath at my back.

But the religious tone of the front yard ended abruptly at the metal gate. There was quite a different scene in Mrs. Hind's backyard. Less hideous though no easier from a mower's point of view. Leaping out of the middle of a neat square of what could have been uninterrupted grass were three large ceramic things. I thought they looked a bit like muddy prehistoric fish, but what they were doing diving out of Mrs. Hind's backyard was beyond me. Three rusted yellow metal chairs, the kind that sit in the same spot for thirty years, usually around an equally rusted table, faced this event, which seemed so unlikely in Mrs. Hind's backyard.

Mrs. Hind herself gave no explanation. When I was done mowing, she'd wave me in for Lorna Doones and lemonade. She paid me promptly. Her hands shook a bit adding a slight echo to each of her movements, but they were strong hands, or had been.

She said very little, she watched me. Sometimes she'd ask me if I had a boyfriend. When I shook my head no, she'd smile and nod her blue head in approval. I'd eat a couple cookies, then stand up and say, "Nice to see you again. Thanks for the cookies. I have to go now." Mrs. Hind would nod her head, "Yes, you'd better go."

The inside of Mrs. Hind's house looked and smelled similar to the others, ranging from molding rugs to cat urine to Evergreen air fresheners that burned my nose and throat. She had the same posed pictures of relatives, except she hung them in circles, three, and she never talked about them. Once, while I sat in the tired gold chair with the green towel folded underneath me, Mrs. Hind caught my eyes drifting into corners across her bookshelves and doilies. She asked with her penciled brow raised, "Are you looking for something?" I quickly answered, "Oh no. Just thinking." I was surprised at my own curiosity. I was looking for something. Not just a clue to her yard, I was looking for some clue to her.

Mrs. Hind went about as though there were nothing unusual, as if there weren't biblical characters rotting disgracefully in her front yard, and prehistoric fish in her back.

I found myself wishing I knew more about Mrs. Hind. I even hoped she would tell me all her old women stories about those relatives hanging on the wall. But Mrs. Hind said nothing, smiling and nodding.

One afternoon, when the leaves were gold and falling, the last day I ever mowed her lawn, Mrs. Hind asked me if I wanted to see her basement. I thought this was strange. Mrs. Hind used a cane and walked slowly. I wondered if she could even get down the stairs to the basement. And if she could, would she be able to get out. I hesitated, but she was already on her way.

With both arms tightly gripping the red pole banister and her cane slung over the back of her neck, she stepped down, one foot at a time. On the second step she stopped to scrape something over the edge of the staircase with her black shoe. It hit the floor with a crack. I noticed the muscles on her forearm, not bulging like mine but definitely used. The light was dim. I followed, waiting on the step just behind her. I was prepared to see almost anything in Mrs. Hind's basement.

As we moved lower I began to smell chemicals, like paint. Then I saw, unfolding along the wall in front of me, bright colors swirling out from a center, like a patchwork snail. But they weren't just colors, they were pictures. Mrs. Hind switched on the lights, with a rather flamboyant motion, and there it was. The basement. Covering the walls were spirals, overflowing onto the ceiling and floor, bending in corners and overlapping. Each spiral was made up of painted scenes. Scene after scene, story after story flowing into a mural that covered the entire basement. I looked closer and recognized some of the faces. They were the same ones that hung in circles in her livingroom. But here they were alive, not stiff and posing, but in the middle of living—crying, sweating, eating, laughing, moving.

Pieces from one lifetime were implanted in others.
There were three mothers rocking babies side by side, each
baby resembling the mother sitting next to her own.
There was an old fashioned farm blending into an almost
modern city. A child on a fat-wheeled, wide-seated bicycle
rode behind a child on a slick seated banana bike who rode
behind a kid in a black 1930s automobile.

I stopped for a while at one scene that pictured two
younger Mrs. Hinds, both leaning over a work table. At
one she was kneading bread dough, at the other a slab of
muddy red clay. This scene flowed into two women sitting in Mrs. Hind's backyard with her, all three eating
what looked like thick slices of brown bread and watching
the prehistoric fish.

When I got to the wall closest to the stairs, I noticed the
lines shaking, as if they had an echo, and some of the
people began to lump out of proportion. Then the pictures
got bigger and bigger, trembling until each stroke of
brush, each color, was a breath—white, orange, blue. At
the tail of the last spiral, just before it stopped abruptly, I
saw myself. There I was in the front yard pushing the lawn
mower up to the feet of Mary as she struggled to hold her
balance in the wind. My long hair was flying across my
face; my faded blue jeans and jean jacket were smeared
with motor grease and grass stains.

I stared at the picture, then looked at Mrs. Hind.

"It's me," I mumbled, stuffing my suddenly shy hands
into the pockets of my grease stained jeans.

"You were working so hard in that wind," she said,
frowning and shaking her head. Then she added, "I suppose it's time to go now."

Mrs. Hind was starting toward the stairs when I saw another, smaller room and asked to go in it. She smiled and

followed. In the room were sculptures of what I assumed to be people she knew. They were figures of women, babies and girls. The one that I remember most, though I looked at it least, was a figure of an older woman reaching for an invisible cupboard or shelf. Her back was rounding, her skin sagged and the fingers of her hand were knobby, curled and wrinkled. It reminded me of the elm I'd built a fort in a few summers before. I used to sit in it and dream until my mother rang the bell for supper. The bark was warm and gritty on my way down. I moved away from the statue quickly.

We went back to the painted room and Mrs. Hind moved with me through the stories, pointing out special scenes with her cane: "He had this twitch in his left cheek that made him look like he was winking. She had hands as big as Montana. That baby spit up carrots on my new blouse, there's the stain." She didn't use many words, as if she knew I would understand. I think I did.

After a while we went upstairs. Gripping her cane and moving slowly she led me straight to the front door. I turned to say something to her like, It's really beautiful, or Thank you for showing me, you're a very good artist. Instead I asked her, "Why do you leave the manger scene in the front yard like that?"

She looked up at me with an odd crinkled face, and whispered, "Because there are fish in the back."

Somehow it made sense to me.

As I opened the door to leave, thinking that the mowing season was over and school was beginning, Mrs. Hind tapped me on the shoulder. When I turned, she hit the floor with her cane, and placed a curled wrinkled finger over her dry purple lips: "Shhh."

I smiled, nodded and left.

By the next summer Mrs. Hind's house was sold. I drove by on my used Honda a couple of times, and stared at the empty lawn that would have been easy to mow. I don't know what happened to her, or her fish, or the manger scene. And I don't know what the new owners did with all her stories in the basement.

TICK

My mother and Peggy and I are in the fourth pew kneeling and begging forgiveness for whatever it is we have done. For example that morning while my mother was in the bathroom putting on her peach foundation I sneaked into the top drawer of her dresser and stole the gold pin shaped like a leaf which she keeps in a box next to the large daisy earrings with the metal petals that poke into your neck. One black eye is peeping out at me from my mother's lobe right now. She wears them with her orange lips and black fuzzy coat, while she begs and the priest chants and I think about how I can't breathe and when will Peggy find a tick.

I like going to church with Peggy because when she gets bored she starts feeling for ticks and she can almost always find one if she feels hard enough. Then she screams and gets weak and someone has to go out with her to take it off and that someone will be me because I'm her best friend and I'm not afraid of ticks and I have longer fingernails. Peggy chews hers to the skin. (Fingernails are important in tick removal to make sure you don't leave the head in which is the worst thing because who wants to go on living, knowing there's a tick head inside you.)

The mass goes on and on, and I'm praying Peggy finds that tick before the long haul of communion. She's feeling her legs now which is where she usually finds them. Meanwhile I sit and kneel and beg with my mouth while my fingers trace the wood grain lines across the back of the pew into heaven—into Lake Sylvia where Peggy and I will go after mass in our new bathing suits.

Then, right in the middle of the long prayer, Peggy lets out this tiny girly scream—"Ehhh"—and clutches my arm like she's going to faint. My mother looks down with her orange lips and I nod and say, "Tick."

We excuse our way around folded hands and knees and I help Peggy, who is limping, through the heavy oak doors into the fresh spring air and sunlight. The tick is on the back of her skinny thigh—it's just a baby so it hasn't got much of her blood yet, but the head is definitely in. (Peggy calls it "tick blood," but I say ticks have none of their own, that's why they steal it.) Peggy leans against the granite wall of the church and holds her breath while I carefully slip my fingernails under the flat brown body which is now dancing around on its neck, if ticks have necks. I pull and Peggy screams, "Did you get the head!" but my mouth is shut tight because even though I'm not afraid of ticks like Peggy, I have a special fear of one sneaking into my belly, fluttering round and round, stealing all of my blood and growing bigger than the ticks on the Carlson dogs that bloat up fat and green until they fall off like oversized grapes.

I squeeze the tick between my thumb and pointer, trying not to think about the tiny legs scratching against my skin as I rush into the church basement and shake it off into the toilet behind the kitchen where they make all those mashed potatoes and mushy green beans. I watch the brown speck twirl round and round until it is sucked into that place I have only seen on movies about rats. (There are only two ways to kill ticks, burning and flushing. I prefer to burn them—who knows what really happens when they go down. There must be millions and zillions of ticks kicking and scratching for blood in the sewer.) I close the lid and mumble heartlessly, "Let it suck on a rat."

Anyway the tick is gone.

Above me I hear the song, "Onward Christian Soldiers," and the steady march of tongues going up for communion. I raise myself slowly off my knees, pass through the dark hallway, up the basement stairs. At the step which leads further up to my pew, I hover, then turn away from the sound and go back through the heavy oak door into the sunlight and air where Peggy is sitting on the soft green grass doing nothing.

I sit next to her, on the grass, doing nothing. That's all we're doing is nothing on a Sunday morning in our paisley white collar dresses and stiff white hats, with the lilacs and the wind. Doing nothing, saying nothing. Because if we say anything it'd have to be, "Should we go back now?" It'd have to be about returning. And if we do anything, anything at all, it'd have to be to get up on our skinny legs and climb back up to the fourth pew, where my mother's orange lips beg, even though those daisy earrings are poking into her neck. And all of a sudden I remember the gold pin, and I wonder if God would save me, if a tick ever got into my stomach.

The Tutu

"I set the clothes I want you to wear today on your bed, Lily, it's time to get ready, Uncle Mark will be here in thirty minutes." There was no answer from Lily's room. She'd been quiet all morning, with that thinking face, smooth as sand dunes and eyes that saw through walls. Her only contribution to breakfast was a mumble through Cheerios and milk, "I know, Mom," when I reminded her of what day it was.

I dressed and knocked at her closed door. "Need any help?" Though she hated to admit it, Lily still had trouble with finishing touches like top buttons and tucking and cuffs.

"No. Don't come in," Lily ordered.

I respected her command. It was going to be a rough day for us all. Though other relatives kept scarce, Lily had been close to her Grandma, my mother, and though she didn't understand death—who does?—Lily knew that Grandma Rose was not going to be stopping by with presents pre-ok'd by me, or reading her books, or bringing peonies from the bulbs they had planted two years ago in Grandma's front lawn.

We'd had many talks about the whole thing. I told Lily that Grandma's spirit would stay with us for a while, and then we'd say goodbye so that she could go on to some other place.

"Where will she go?" Lily asked.

"Anywhere she wants."

"Then why doesn't she stay here?"

"Well... because she's been here for a long time and now she gets to go somewhere else."

It was a petrifying conversation. I did my best on short notice.

"Lily, honey, hurry up. We only have ten minutes," I said, ignoring how little that meant to her. I walked to the front window in my autumn-colored slacks and mourned over the apples on our tree. As I watched, one fell to the ground where others laid rotting, pecked with bird holes. The three of us would have picked them this week; Mom and Lily would be baking pies and apple butter now. "Remember, Mom, no sugar, she'll get enough of that at school."

Oh, Rose, I am going to miss you, I thought. Even the fights about Lily's heathen lifestyle, not to mention my own, and her unsuitable wardrobe; "Why don't you dress her up nice the way I dressed you! Oh you used love to wear the prettiest little pink dresses and matching outfits." I'd remind her that all I had were pretty little dresses and matching outfits that I couldn't get dirty or dream in.

But today was Grandma's day, so I had carefully picked out, for myself and Lily, respectable attire—one of my more conventional outfits and one of Lily's few dresses. All the relatives would be there, and family friends, most of whom had never met Lily or seen me since I had been scandalously and willfully inseminated.

I heard Lily's door open slowly, "shhhing" against the worn carpet in a vow of secrecy, then her light footsteps. I turned to her with a reassuring smile.

"Oh, Lily. No!"

In seven minutes my brother would pull up in his new SAAB with Great Aunt Jane, my mother's sister, and Uncle Bert strapped into the back seat. And there stood Lily—in her green leotard, red patent leather shoes and the hot pink tutu we'd bought at a thrift shop for play. The tutu was full and wafted out below her knees, some of the lace hanging lower than that. She looked like something that might fly across the room, or swagger.

"Lily, you cannot wear that to the funeral. You can wear the dress I laid out, or... or the white pants with the leotard if you want but not that."

My daughter's brown eyes which matched my own which matched my mother's, sped around the room, as if the words to convince me, to explain, were hidden in the walls and furniture. Her fingers tugged at the lace.

"I have to wear this," she whispered.

The clock on my wrist ticked like sharp teeth nipping at my heels. I tried to stay calm, like a good mother.

"I know you want to wear that, but I just can't let you... it's not the right place. Remember Cousin Mary's wedding? How I told you that people wear certain kinds of clothes? Well, funerals are like that too."

God, where was the book to tell me how to do this. I could see my words were having no effect.

"Lily, you can wear the tutu tomorrow, or the next day I PROMISE. You can wear it for the rest of your life— BUT NOT TO GRANDMA'S FUNERAL!"

I sat down. This was getting scary. Lily stood stiff as a doll, staring through me out the window.

"I am," she said, barely opening her tight little mouth which I suddenly had the urge, my first, to slap. The way my mother had slapped mine—not hard, not often, but lasting.

"Enough! You've got exactly two minutes to change,

young lady, now get in there and put on that yellow dress!"

A voice that wasn't my own, yet familiar, echoed in my ears and startled a tiny squeak out of Lily who jumped and ran into the bathroom. She fumbled with the lock, which we never used, but I wedged my body in first. I picked her up and carried her into her bedroom, tutu scratching my face, Lily's screams cutting into my eardrum.

"Lily stop this!" I squeezed her tight.

"You're hurting me! You're hurting me!" She choked, pinching my heart with eyes that looked up at me as if I'd grown fangs. It was the look I used to give my mother. The one that said "I hate you!" and "Who are you?" at the same time.

I slid to the bed. Lily jerked away from me and buried her face in the pillow which Grandma had made her— shaped like a two legged cat. A horn honked at the front of the house. Lily's sobs came out in puffs like they'd climbed a hill and finally made it to the top only to be pushed down the other end. When she was two and hated putting her snow suit on I could drape her across my lap and wedge her arms and legs through those endless holes. She'd go limp. Now I glanced over at this other child, whose extremities had sprouted out from nowhere.

I don't want a limp child, I thought, not today. But I had to do something—I was her mother.

For a moment I considered threatening to leave her at home, but with Lily I might have had to do it and I didn't want to chance her growing up in a perpetual state of denial because she'd missed seeing her Grandma's body lowered into the ground.

Three more polite honks poked at my shoulder.

"Lily, don't you think Grandma would want you to wear the yellow dress?"

She twisted her nose into the cat's stomach, her short, blunt cut hair wagged.

"I'll buy you a Cabbage Patch. . . "

I'd been holding out for two years. My skin was growing scales and green slime. If I looked in the mirror I was sure I'd see the face of a frustrated young mother, my own; and that girl on the bed would be me.

She was quiet now, except for an occasional shudder that rippled down her body like wind on a leaf.

"Lily. Is there anything I can say to change your mind?"

I wilted over her legume legs. Her head wagged, then lifted glassy eyes to mine, like a prisoner pleading for her life. The horn honked and I sighed. A mother's sigh, preparing for the onslaught of eyebrows, mouths and chins questioning my right to Motherhood, my right to Daughterhood, my sanity, and pitying poor Lily—the innocent victim of the 1980's sperm bank.

"OK, kid. Let's go say bye to Grandma."

My brother glanced at Lily once, then at me, then at the road.

"Quite a dress you've got on there, Lily."

Lily jumped into the back seat and buckled herself in between Great Aunt Jane and Uncle Bert, who were properly clad in nondescript clothing.

"OK! Let's go!"

Lily cheered, as if we were going to a birthday party; the pink tutu sprang up nearly to her chin, as if filled with helium, or candy, like a pinata. She watched houses and buildings go by, jiggling her ankles and asking "Are we there yet?" at every red light. "No, not yet," I'd answer like a normal mother, talking to a normal child. The rest of the passengers were loudly silent, and, I imagined, making grave faces at the back of my head. At least I wouldn't have to see them again until someone else died, I thought.

An hour and fifty-one are-we-there-yets later Mark pulled into one of the parking spaces reserved for heavy mourners, and before Great Aunt Jane could reach the handle I heard the snap of steel and Lily bounded out the door and up the sidewalk, the too big, too bright tutu flouncing up and down like a used float in a parade.

"Come on Mom!" She waved me on excitedly as she bounced and flounced her way among the somber dark legs of others who had come to pay their last respects. Lily was a wild flower in a dead forest.

I clutched my wad of Kleenex and followed, noting the eyebrows and mouths and chins. But also a few tired grateful smiles. She was well-loved, my mother, I thought.

"Excuse me, I have to keep up with my child."

I held my head as high as I could without losing sight of Lily.

Once through the funeral home doors into the carpeted airless quiet, Lily's tutu flattened a bit, but I could see something bubbling under her skin, and I wondered what was going on in her child's head. Through my tears I watched her red shoes weave between rows of relatives, up to the open casket where my mother laid peacefully. Lily hopped onto the kneeling bench. The room held its breath. My heart thumped with pride and terror as I watched Lily grab handfuls of bright pink lace and hold it over my mother's waxen face.

"Look, Grandma!" she bursted out. "I wore a pretty pink dress just like you told me to in the dream. It's just exactly the same color as our flowers we planted in your front yard!"

Spring Cleaning

Every spring, on the first of April, Sheila cleaned her house. She started in her bedroom, cleaned her way through the bathroom and closets and kitchen. Then finally into the living room.

It was on this day, the day of fools, that Sheila moved the couch away from the wall in order to vacuum up the dust and break the cobwebs that had gathered there over the long winter. And it was there, behind the couch, that Sheila found things. Last year it had been a blue comb with three missing teeth. The year before it had been the tiny screwdriver she used to fasten the bows of her glasses when they came loose. The year before that it had been a Canadian nickel. Sheila would pick them up, dust them off, and return them to their proper places. She put the comb into the first bathroom drawer, the screwdriver into the little side pouch of her glasses case, and the nickel into her purse. Odd things, like bolts and washers whose source remained unknown, were kept in a box labeled SURPRISES FROM UNDER THE COUCH.

There were not many surprises in Sheila's life, and so she was grateful for the small ones. She had been born in the house, and was now quite sure she would die in the house, though her hopes at one time had been different.

When Sheila was young, before her mother got sick and died, she joined a travel club. For two years she ordered brochures and planned her travels to special places. France, Russia, India, Australia, Japan. . . . Each spring would bring new people and new scenery and new weather. Home would be in many little rooms all over the world.

So went Sheila's dreams.

Then something happened inside her. Her mother got sick and Sheila stayed in the house to take care of her. And when her mother died, Sheila suddenly knew that she was never going to leave this house. Except to go to work, or to church on Sunday mornings, or to buy groceries. And with this realization came a feeling of numb safety.

So Sheila packed the travel brochures away in a box with no label, and started to grow old. Spring after spring.

This spring the house was dustier than ever, or so she thought, as she pounded, scrubbed, and swept her way to the couch. Sheila pushed on one end, and then the other. What had once been an easy task was getting harder, and Sheila could feel her back and legs ache as if the bones were rusted shut. Finally, when the couch was far enough out from the wall, Sheila peeked her head over the top. And there on the floor was a letter.

"Oh," she said to herself. "A letter."

She picked it up and stared at the beautiful stamp. It was postmarked Paris, France. Sheila frowned. Did she know anyone in Paris, France? No. She didn't know anyone from anywhere, she thought.

"Well, it must be a mistake," she mumbled to herself. "It must be someone else's letter."

And yet it was her name printed on the front, and this was her house, and her living room. Sheila sat down and opened the letter. It read:

Dear Sheila,

Hope spring cleaning is going well. I am having a wonderful time in Paris, eating my way from café to café. The colors here remind me of dreams lost. The people seem crabby, not like they say in those brochures, but once you can speak the language with some grace the Parisians can be friendly. I really do think you should come someday— you'd love it! And it would be good for you to get out of that house; some place entirely different. We're not getting younger you know! Anyway, just wanted to drop you a note, wish you well and let you know that I'm thinking of you. Hope you like the photos I've sent. Don't work too hard.

Love, Nan

Sheila read the letter again. Nan? Did she know a Nan? She looked at the pictures. The buildings and scenery reminded her of those in the brochure she'd ordered on France. Sheila felt a closed place inside her cracking open. She shut her eyes and imagined being in Paris. Then opened them quickly.

That week she went through all of her school year books and photo albums, but she could find no memory of a woman named Nan. After a short while Sheila began to feel silly, and afraid.

"The whole thing is ridiculous," she told herself. "Somebody has played a joke on you."

She stuck the letter in the box labeled SURPRISES FROM UNDER THE COUCH, and went on with her daily life. She went to work; she went to church; and she bought groceries.

But the next spring, when Sheila moved the couch, there was another letter, postmarked USSR—Moscow. It read:

Dear Sheila,

Decided to spend this spring in Moscow. Wish you could see the color of the Russian sky, pictures just don't capture the beauty. I spent a whole day staring at Saint Basil's; remember, it's the one you liked so much in the brochure? You thought it looked like a fairy's castle, and it does. Though it is a communist country and I don't approve of communism, the people are friendly and helpful. (But the lines are terrible!) I can only stay for a month, then on to new people, new scenery, new weather. Someday we'll just have to connect! Happy cleaning.

Love, Nan.

Sheila read the words and looked at the pictures until the room was dark. Then she sat there, still, with the paper in her lap. At dawn she pushed the couch into place, went into her room and took out her box of travel brochures. She put them in a new box, along with the letters, labeled LETTERS FROM UNDER THE COUCH. AND MY BROCHURES.

She kept this box close to her bed.

Every spring, for the next five years, Sheila got a letter from a new place: India, Australia, Japan. . . . She stopped questioning why or how or who this friend could be. She believed in her; grew fond of her. It was as if they had been friends all of her life. Sheila began to dream again, quietly, alone, at night.

The sixth spring, Sheila could barely move the couch by herself. If it weren't for the letter, she might have given up. Slowly, she pushed and tugged, until the couch was a small way out from the wall. Sheila peeked her head over the top, but, except for the dust and cobwebs, the space on the floor was empty. Sheila got on her hands and knees and raked the carpet with her fingers. Nothing. She started to look everywhere—behind the other chairs, behind shelves, in corners. Her hands shook. She sobbed and shouted until her throat went dry. There was no letter.

Sheila lay on the floor and let the rest of the day pass into night. Finally, she picked herself up, dusted herself off, and pushed the couch back to the wall, leaving the usual crack. Then she got out a pretty pink piece of paper and matching envelope. She wrote:

Dear Nan,

This is Sheila in America. I didn't get a letter from you this year and I am wondering if you are OK. Are you sick? Did you lose my address? Spring is nice here, like always, and the house is all cleaned, but I really miss your letter. Please write one soon if you can.

Love, Sheila

She put three stamps on it, then slipped it behind the couch.

After waiting one week, Sheila moved the couch to check. Her letter was still there, and no other had arrived. For the next two months she checked behind the couch once a week... then once a month. ...

Finally she stopped checking, and left the couch alone.

Winter came with icy winds and piles of snow that leaned against the house. Sheila lay in bed with cold after cold, feeling very old. She had packed the box labeled LETTERS FROM UNDER THE COUCH. AND MY BROCHURES away, and began referring to herself as "foolish old woman," though she was not, in fact, very old or very foolish.

During one long spell of fever, while Sheila's skin burned down to the bone and the winds blew, she wrote another letter on pink paper to her friend, telling her how sick she felt, how lonely, and that she was sure she would soon die, and so this was good bye.

She dropped the letter behind the couch, but could not find the energy to move it.

Slowly, the snow melted and warmer winds brought spring. Sheila did not die, and on April first, she got up out of her bed to clean. She forced her thoughts away from the couch and letters, as she pounded, scrubbed, and swept her way through the house.

"It was nonsense," she repeated to herself. "Silly dreams. You should be content with the life you've got right here, and with this fine house your mother left you."

She hired a neighbor boy to move the couch. Sheila stood ready with her vacuum.

"Just a few feet out from the wall, that's right."

Suddenly the boy bent over and picked something up.

"Hey, a letter!" he said, holding it out. "Wow, it's from Africa. Do you know someone in Africa?"

Sheila's eyes lit up as she grabbed the letter out of the boy's hands, then patted his head and gave him a dollar.

"Don't you want me to move the couch back?"

"Oh, it doesn't matter. It's all right. You go on."

The letter was warm in her hands. When the boy was gone, Sheila sat on the couch and slowly opened it. Her heart jumped as she read:

My Dearest Sheila,

I am so sorry I couldn't write last spring. Was near death with malaria here in an African hospital. Took me all winter to recuperate. Thank you much for your lovely letters. So you had a rough winter too? I'm very worried about you. But listen! I have a wonderful idea! I am just now packing for Greece where it will be warm and sunny, with air easy to breathe for us aging ladies who like to travel.

You join me (I've sent the ticket!) and from there we'll go
back to Paris—Oh, I'd love to show you Paris!

I'll meet you at the airport—I know you'll come, and
we'll have a great time. See you soon.

Love, Nan

The next day, Sheila pushed the couch against the wall,
packed her bags, locked the house, and left. No one in
America ever saw her again, but eventually a distant rela-
tive sold her house to a middle-aged widow whose name
was Mary. On April first, during her first spring cleaning,
Mary moved the couch away from the wall and found a
letter in a pink envelope. It read:

Dear Mary,

Hello! Just want to send you some pictures and let you
know I am spending the winter in Bolivia. I really like the
mountains, and everything is nice. Hope spring cleaning is
going on OK.

Love, Sheila

Julie Blackwomon   Nona Caspers

About the Authors

Julie Blackwomon has been published in several journals as well as the anthologies *Lesbian Poetry*, *Lesbian Fiction*, and *Home Girls: A Black Feminist Anthology*. She lives in Philadelphia and is currently at work on a novel.

Nona Caspers's short fiction and poetry have appeared in journals such as *Hurricane Alice*, *Plainswoman*, *Evergreen Chronicles*, and *Negative Capability* and in the anthology *Word of Mouth*. She is currently residing in the San Francisco Bay Area.

OTHER LESBIAN TITLES FROM SEAL PRESS